Serenade/Saga

Anna's Rocking Chair

ELAINE WATSON

I Have Chosen Right . .

Susan told herself, with a burst of a[...] or her kind, slow-spoken husband.

"I can't wait until we get to Michigan, Abe! Did you know the only time I've ever stayed on a farm was last summer when I went to help Olive with the baby?"

Finally Abe spoke. "Well, Susan, you'll have to wait a little longer, I guess." He turned to look at her, apparently aware of his blunt words. Then he smiled—a slow, intimate smile. "But there'll be a surprise for you, too, when we get home. Kind of a wedding surprise. Your ma and pa thought I'd forgot, didn't they? Well, I was taught some manners, you know. And besides, I wanted to buy you a present anyway, manners or not."

His slow, lazy smile made her heart beat faster. "Oh, Abe, we'll have a fine trip. Reverend Schneider said, 'This is a grave move, my child, going into that wild land to start a wedded life.' How wrong they all are!"

Susan looked back at the white-painted house where she had spent her nineteen years. Her mother, head bent, was wiping her eyes with the corner of her calico apron, and her shoulders were shaking.

Susan's serenity was shattered. She remembered exclaiming on her return from visiting Olive, "Mama, I've found the man I intend to marry."

"He's from a good family?"

"Well—he's a Bavarian."

"A man who speaks Low Dutch? You can't be serious about this attachment!"

Now, watching her mother weep, for the first time Susan felt a slight twinge of concern.

Karen Wood
May, 1986

ANNA'S ROCKING CHAIR

Elaine Watson

Serenade/Saga
BOOKS
of the Zondervan Publishing House
Grand Rapids, Michigan

ANNA'S ROCKING CHAIR
© Copyright 1984 by The Zondervan Corporation
Grand Rapids, Michigan

Library of Congress Cataloging in Publication Data
Watson, Elaine.
    Anna's rocking chair.

    I. Title.
PS3573.A852A83   1984   813'.54   83-19673
ISBN 0-310-46482-X

Book Designer: Kim Koning
Edited by Anne Severance and Nancye Willis

Printed in the United States of America

85   86   87   88   89 / 10   9   8   7   6   5   4   3   2

For Bill

For Dave, Peggy, and Doug

Diane and Darryl

PROLOGUE

SUSAN HAD MARRIED beneath her. Everyone said so.

Susan's father gave a qualified blessing only because Abe's little farm in Michigan—far out in what seemed like wilderness to civilized people in Milwaukee—bordered on the large government grant where Susan's sister Olive and her elderly husband lived.

Susan's mother planned her daughter's trousseau the same way her own mother had planned for each of her daughters long ago in Prussia. But her set lips spoke volumes, and her silence screamed disapproval.

And Susan's brother Karl, writing from a Lutheran seminary in Berlin, advised against the marriage, too.

All Bavarian peasants are ignorant and superstitious. I have heard they entertain ghosts in their bedrooms. In fact, sister, if I believed a malevolent spirit could exist anywhere on this earth, I am sure it would be found not in the lofty chambers of an ancient castle like those I have

7

seen near Hamburg. It would be lurking in the bleak little hut of a Bavarian peasant. This kind of marriage, my sister, is not for you.

Susan ignored her family's misgivings. She had none of her own.

At first.

CHAPTER 1

EARLY ON THE MORNING following their simple wedding ceremony in her mother's front parlor, Susan and Abe began their long journey to Abe's farm. For nearly a year Susan had pictured Abe's farm as a sort of haven. But there had been just a few times, too, when that remote farmhouse, shrouded in Michigan's swampy mists, loomed a little frightening, from the corners of her dreams. Since Abe had come to Milwaukee to marry her, though, her happiness had driven those fragments of disquiet far away.

Over a breakfast of spicy sausages and raised pancakes covered with brown sugar, Susan's father said, "Well, children, I wish you a safe trip. I won't be able to see you off, I fear. After the vows were spoken last night Cousin Amos told me about old Colonel Schulte's estate. They're settling it today, and the earlier I get a bid on that choice piece of land, the better."

He sat erect, the way he always did, his gaunt face atop his small frame a picture of stern, calculating efficiency.

Then he turned to Abe. "And do savages still threaten our settlers in your remote Michigan wilderness in these days, Abraham?" he asked. "And wolves? Have you managed to drive back the wolves?"

"Oh, Papa!" cried Susan. "Olive never writes us about Indians or wild animals. You didn't ask Joseph questions like those when he took Olive to *his* farm in Michigan!"

Her father looked at her in a way that always stopped what he felt was impertinence in any of his daughters. But with her brother Karl, Susan noticed, he was tolerant—even respectful.

Susan closed her mouth. Abe, sticking his fork into another fat sausage and bringing it to his plate, said nothing, but when she glanced sidelong at him, Susan was startled to see the corners of his lips turn up and what looked like a gleam of fun light his brown eyes. Could he be *laughing* at Papa?

"Milwaukee is growing up around the land Susan's mother and I bought when we came to this country twenty-five years back," her father told Abe. "And we've done quite well. I hope your investments are sound ones, too, Abraham."

"I believe they are, Mr. Faust. My farm is on rich soil," Abe said. Obviously he was unruffled by her father's querulous, probing questions that always created an atmosphere of tension whenever he was at home.

10

Susan knew that for her father his first wife's grave in the Old Country and the children from that marriage were now distant memories. The only reminder was Karl's lodging with his half-sister in Berlin while he studied for the ministry. Susan did not miss Karl. But she would miss her younger sister Laura, who was living with their Aunt Elviry a few miles north, in Milwaukee, and attending a Lutheran school for young ladies.

Both Susan and Olive had been students there, too, where they had learned, in addition to music and letters and religion, to honor their father and mother.

So now Susan kept her mouth closed, biding her time until she could leave forever the table her parents had always dominated. She quickly helped her mother and the hired "girl"—an elderly spinster from a neighboring farm—clear away the dishes. Then, as soon as she could, she ran back to her room for her bonnet and cape.

When Susan helped Abe lift a small trunk and her embroidered carpetbag—a wedding present from Aunt Elviry—into the shiny black cutter, she erased the turmoil of the past week from her mind. She took one last look around her. The great fir tree that shadowed her parents' handsome frame house had provided shade for summer picnics. Now the snow on its drooping branches was reflected in her mother's sparkling windows.

She loved to ride in the cutter this time of year. The air was no longer bitter, but the smooth runners on a late February snow crust still made for a lively trip.

Susan was eager to travel alone with her new husband through a promise of early spring sunshine. She glanced at Abe, who was checking the harness fastenings. The leather was worn and gray. The old harness had been hanging behind the last stalls in the barn, since it was used only for occasional journeys like this one. Her father kept the good harness for himself. She felt a burst of affection for her kind, slow-spoken husband.

Again she told herself she had chosen right.

"I can't wait until we get to Michigan, Abe," she began, with a smile. "I feel like a pioneer! Papa said," she mimicked his sigh, "'Riding all that way through these country roads is dangerous for a woman. But your Uncle Adolph wants that carved chest, and I guess he's entitled to it. And it's got to have special care taken. A strong man like your *Abraham*,'" she smiled again, "'will be more trustworthy, I suppose, than some old fool working for the train crew.'"

With a satisfied grin, Susan said a silent good-by to her father.

Her mood changed. "Did you know," she went on, "the only time I've ever stayed on a farm was last summer when I went to help Olive with the baby?"

Abe straightened the reins over the horse's back. Finally he spoke. "Well, Susan, you'll have to wait a little longer, I guess." He turned to look at her, apparently aware of his blunt words. Then he smiled—a slow, intimate smile. "But I guess there'll be a surprise for you, too, when we get home. Kind of a wedding surprise."

Susan took a deep breath. "I knew you would get me a wedding present, Abe."

12

He continued to watch her face. "Your Ma and Pa thought I'd forgot, didn't they? Well, I was taught some manners, you know. And besides," he went on, "I wanted to buy you a present anyway, manners or not."

His slow, lazy smile made her heart beat faster.

At once the world was right again. "Oh, Abe," she said, laughing, "we'll have such a fine trip to our farm. Our own farm. Even Reverend Schneider, after he finished marrying us last night, took me aside and he said"—she drew her mouth down and looked over imaginary spectacles—"'This is a grave move, my child, going into that wild land in Michigan with Mr. Hesse to start a wedded life. A grave move.' How wrong they all are!"

Susan watched him as he stood with his big farmer's hands on the mare's face, stroking gently so the horse would get to know her unfamiliar driver. "There, there, Nellie," he murmured. Abe's tie was askew above a stiff wing collar. He moved awkwardly in his new black suit and greatcoat.

Suddenly she recalled what Karl had written about Bavarians and their ghosts. "Abe," she said, laughing at the absurdity of it, "do *you* have a ghost in your parlor? My brother says you probably believe in ghosts!"

Abe's hands on Nellie's face stopped abruptly. He did not turn around. Then, with a slight shake of his head, he chuckled briefly. But the choked sound seemed forced.

"That's a kind of fool remark, I'd say, Susan," he muttered. "Your brother made a fool remark."

A little puzzled, but determined not to let anything

bother her today, Susan decided it might be best not to pursue that subject just now.

"Of course," she agreed. "After we get settled, and Mama sends my piano to me, we will have such a lovely home! My piano will shoo any old ghost out of our parlor!"

Susan's mother called from the porch, "Susan!"

At once she turned to obey. But this time she walked slowly instead of hurrying the way she had been taught to do since childhood.

I'm a woman now, she thought, *a married woman. I will act like one.*

Her mother's stern face—with its clear blue eyes and the pink and white skin of her ancestors—softened not at all.

"You needn't take off your boots, Susan. Just stay there on the steps. I have a list of things I want Adolph to get for me in Chicago before he brings the cutter back. There are some supplies I'll need for my garden. I can't find them here in South Milwaukee. You'd better look at my list and buy some things for yourself, too. Don't forget crocks, now, child. That's pretty wild country you're going into. Not so settled on that little back road, I expect, as on the road where Olive lives. It won't be easy for you to get to the village."

She paused, handing Susan a folded paper, and— just for a moment—she held her daughter's fingers in her own.

Then she went on briskly, "You'll want to plant a good garden with plenty of cucumbers and cabbages and carrots and potatoes on Abraham's land. And put them away for winter."

On our *land,* Susan told herself, nodding meanwhile in agreement.

"Mama," she said aloud, "I think we're ready. Don't bother to put on your boots. And Mama, Abe will have a wedding present for me! A surprise! Maybe he bought it in Chicago a couple of days ago when he came through on the railway train."

She looked at her mother one last time, standing on the porch with her arms folded across her wide, shawl-covered stomach. This was the picture she planned to remember.

Abe came up behind her. He took off his felt hat, and the breeze lifted his dark ringlets. "Well, we'll say good-by," he said. He put out his hand to Susan's mother. "I'll take care of Susan, Mrs. Faust. It's best to get started now. That land of mine is waiting for spring sunshine and spring planting."

That land of ours, Susan corrected Abe in her mind.

Her mother shook Abe's hand briefly. She said only, "Mind that chest now, won't you. It takes a strong man to handle it right. Don't let Adolph try to do it alone."

Susan wrapped a black shawl around the shoulders of her green alpaca cape. Green set off her tawny hair and white skin, so she had chosen the prettiest and warmest green cape she could find when she had shopped in Milwaukee for her trousseau.

She happily decided to store all memories of her childhood into a remote corner of her mind as she watched Abe climb into the seat next to her and slap the reins on the horse's rump. The runners of the cutter jolted out of a frozen rut.

15

When they turned down the narrow, poplar-lined path that led to the road, Susan looked back. Dark green shutters contrasted with the white-painted house where she had spent her nineteen years.

Her mother, head bent, was leaning against a post on the porch. Never before had Susan seen her lean against anything. She was wiping her eyes with the corner of her calico apron, and her shoulders were shaking.

Susan's serenity was shattered.

"Mama," she remembered exclaiming on her return from visiting Olive the summer before, "I have found the man I intend to marry!"

Susan and her mother had been sitting in rocking chairs that night on the wide porch running across the front of their house. The evening air was soft around them as they rocked and exchanged news of Michigan and Milwaukee.

"Well, well, Susan," her mother had replied, "there's plenty of time for that. Is he a rich farmer from Prussia like Joseph? Or maybe a minister's son from the village? I do hope Olive introduced you to the right sort of neighbors."

"Oh, yes, he *is* the right sort. He's a good, kind man, and he has some education, too. We had such fun together on Sunday nights at Olive's house."

"But he's from a good family?"

"Well, I'm sure he is. But his Mama and Papa are dead. And his sister Anna died last year—in that little house where he lives. He's all alone, and he misses Anna terribly. Olive told me he nearly lost his mind when she died. I think he needs me, Mama."

Her mother had looked alarmed. "Was there an inheritance? Or maybe there will be money from property in Prussia?"

"Well," Susan recalled how hard it had been to say the next words, "he's a Bavarian, I think."

"A man who speaks Low Dutch? Oh, my child, you can't be serious about this attachment!"

Now, watching her mother weep, for the first time Susan felt a slight twinge of concern.

But then she stored the memory of her mother away, too. She set her lips tight and turned her eyes toward the spring sunshine.

CHAPTER 2

"I'M SO GLAD Uncle Adolph wanted that precious old chest of his brought right to his door in Chicago. The cutter is more fun than the train," Susan began. At home she seldom was included in adult conversations, but with Abe she felt free to chatter. Her father did not allow idle chatter.

"Well, he'll have to fill your Ma's list and get right back. See over there—the snow's starting to melt already. It's kind of a fool trip this time of the year, anyhow," he grumbled. "And hard on a horse, even a big strong mare like this one is. Like as not we're going to have to stop and rest her a good many times."

Susan turned to feast her eyes on him for the first time since she had gone to the train station with her father to pick him up two days earlier. She laughed. "Where did you learn to talk like that, Abe?" she asked. "Is that the way all those Michigan Low Dutch peasants talk?"

18

She thought he would laugh, too. She remembered the fun they had had together, when she had kept house for Olive during her sister's last confinement —their games of checkers and blindman's bluff at church parties, their evenings with popcorn and cider in Olive's big front yard among young folks from neighboring farms.

Their long walks down lonely lanes, with his arm around her and her head on his shoulder.

But now she saw a slow flush rise in Abe's cheek. "I went to the high school for a couple of years when I lived with Mr. Spencer, you know," he said. "Even Anna went to high school." He did not look at her.

Susan felt an urge to reach out and hug him, but she did not. She was not sure what his reaction would be. The night before in her own bedroom he had only put his arms around her and held her for a moment before he turned down the wick on the oil lamp.

"You must be pretty tired," he had said. And then he had gone to sleep.

So now she said nothing. Never again, though, would she ridicule his origins. After all, she had spent the past winter trying to convince her family such things did not really matter in this country.

Abe was bringing nothing into the family. And he was taking out a carefully trained wife who should be helping at home or at least settling near her aging parents and little sister. Susan's mother had apprenticed her as a seamstress for a year with old Mrs. Kuhl on the next street, after she completed her schooling in Milwaukee. "And all that money spent to train a woman just to scrub floors and dig potatoes for a peas-

19

ant!'' her mother had complained to her Aunt Elviry at Christmas, when she had thought Susan was upstairs. Susan remembered how the word *peasant* had hurt her ears then, and knew how Abe must have felt when she used it. Somehow she must cheer him up.

"Abe," she ventured, "tell me what Chicago is like. I wanted to take the railway train the whole way last year, but Mama talked me into that old trip across Lake Michigan. Everybody was sick to their stomachs, and the steamer was so dirty. Olive's husband says it's a better way to go, though, so that convinced Mama."

"You'll have to start calling Olive's husband 'Joseph' now that your Ma says we're going to live with them for a few weeks," Abe advised, his face relaxing a little.

Susan laughed, glad that she had started him on another subject. "But he's so *old*. He's really a second or third cousin of Papa's, you know. I feel more like calling him 'Uncle Joseph'!"

"Old and rich," he countered, quietly.

"He plans to go back home to Prussia with the money he makes here," Susan said, "and take his family with him. 'Or,'" she mimicked Joseph's wheezy voice, "'our sons can continue in their own way here on my good, rich land,' he told Mama when he came courting Olive. His first wife died back home, years ago."

"Back *home?*" Abe murmured.

Startled out of a concept she had not questioned before, Susan let Abe's remark pass. She quickly went on to a new subject.

20

"And Joseph's sick, too. I saw him throwing up behind the corn cribs lots of times last summer. I told Olive, but she said he has a nervous stomach." Olive had said that in such a decisive way Susan did not speak of it again.

Abe chuckled. "Susan, you're a grown-up woman. Don't you know what's wrong with old Joseph? That's pretty hard cider he puts down every year. And those long trips to town wouldn't be all that long either if the saloon closed a little earlier."

Susan caught her breath. "Whatever will Mama say when she hears about that? She thought Olive made such a good match!" Then she caught her breath again, knowing her remark might imply she herself had failed to make a good match. Her mind darted about to find another subject to soothe Abe's feelings once more.

But this time he fooled her. He smiled slowly, his face lighting up as he sought her eyes. "Let's just forget about all those folks for a while, Susan. What pretty trinkets are you going to buy for yourself down there in Chicago?"

Susan laughed again, ruefully, remembering the crocks her mother had told her to get. She glanced at the bank of what had begun to look like spring rain clouds on the horizon and saw they were really snow-laden. Their safe trip, and even Adolph's swift return to Milwaukee with the cutter, seemed assured.

"I've got a list!" she said.

By the time they stopped to let the horse rest once again and to eat their potatoes that had been taken from the oven that morning—they were still slightly warm—the new bank of clouds had risen higher in the southwest. The day grew gray then. The sparkling ice of the morning was long gone, and dark trees along the road seemed to close in before and behind them while Abe cracked the reins to hurry their tiring horse.

Because she became anxious, Susan was silent. She saw that Abe, too, watched the cloud bank as it rose above the treetops. With the onset of darkness, she remembered her father's stories of wolves that lay in wait by forest roads—hungry wolves in late winter— and of sleighs and cutters that returned home without their passengers. Susan and Abe met no other people on the road for the last hour of the day, and loneliness closed in, along with the dark and the forest. She began to think about the safety of the train they could have taken.

"Abe," she ventured, fearing the trend of her solitary thoughts, "*are* there wolves in the forests of Michigan?"

He glanced at her through the gloom. Then he tucked the gray knit lap robe tighter around her. He smiled. "Don't worry, Susan," he said. "No wolf will bother you, I promise you, not even in the wilds of Michigan."

She longed to have him put his arm around her, but he did not. His words gave her comfort, though.

Finally they came upon a shuttered farmhouse and its barn in a patch of cleared land, and then an old log church. Susan realized her heart had been pounding and her ears, straining for the howl of wolves. Now she put her hand on her breast to quiet it and took a deep breath.

Thank You. Thank You, she prayed.

The next building was a hotel Adolph had recommended. It turned out to be a log house, hugging the edge of the road and stretching back into the forest. Above the door its cracked signboard, lighted by a faint candle enclosed in glass, swung in the rising wind. On the sign words in white paint spelled out "Grand Hotel."

"These must be English people," exclaimed Susan. "Look at the way they spell!"

"I don't care if they're Rooshan," growled Abe. "The horse needs a rest, and so do I."

And so do I, thought Susan, *and some comforts of a hotel, too.* Susan's mother had raised her daughters to keep their own counsel about bodily functions, so she felt she could never—never as long as she lived with him—discuss such things with Abe.

The front door of the hotel swung open and a tall man wearing a fur coat and an old fur cap silently motioned Abe around to the stable at the back, and, without a word to Susan either, lifted her carpetbag out of the cutter and jerked his head toward the door. Susan followed him, tottering on her cold feet. He took her directly up a steep flight of stairs to an attic room. He set his kerosene lamp next to an unlighted one on the walnut dresser. The dresser was the only piece of furniture in the room, except for a large walnut bed set against a far wall under the eaves and covered with a patchwork quilt. The man raised the dirty lamp chimney, lighted one wick with the other, and, still without a word, shuffled across the braided rug and back down the stairs.

23

As soon as she could Susan, too, left the bleak room.

She found Abe already sitting at a long table covered with a cracked white oilcloth. He was writing their name in a ledger. "Mr. and Mrs. Abraham Hesse, Michigan," he wrote.

He smiled at her briefly when she sat down next to him and looked at the ledger. Her mind was foggy from fatigue, but she grinned back at him. "Mrs. Abraham Hesse," she whispered. Her hand wanted to touch Abe's arm, but her mind kept her fingers, tightly closed, in her lap. Her parents never touched in public.

Then he and Susan ate hot potato soup and white bread in the dim, bare dining room. The wind howled outside and stray breezes slipped through chinks between the logs in the wall behind them. The smell of dumplings and onions in the soup mingled with a strong odor from the kerosene lamp.

No one else was in the room except for an old woman who served them. She was wrapped in a dark shawl and wore a black wool scarf on her head.

They were so weary they hardly spoke.

As soon as they got to the bedroom, Abe sat on the bed with his back to Susan and took off his suitcoat, vest, and shirt. He slipped on the striped flannel nightshirt she had glimpsed only briefly the night before in the dark of her own room. He removed his boots and trousers and got into bed.

Glancing briefly toward her, he said, "Susan, I'm bushed!" Then he quickly pulled the covers over his head, just the way he had on their wedding night.

24

Almost immediately she heard him begin to snore softly.

Susan sat on her side of the bed, looking at the heap of patchwork quilt for a moment. She shivered in the stale, icy air.

Then she blew out the light.

She took off her skirt and her shirtwaist, drew on her white flannel gown—which she had trimmed with pink and blue ribbons—pulled the pins from the bun at the back of her head, and crept between the two feather ticks. She sank deep into the chill ticking next to Abe.

Susan's body ached from the long, cold ride, but she lay awake listening to the rush of the wind and to a mouse scurrying in an attic space farther along under the eaves. She choked back a wave of homesickness for the house she had been eager to leave only a few hours before.

Never again, she vowed, *will we go to sleep without speaking, no matter how tired we are. Abe has lived alone too long. I must not feel sorry for myself. I must teach him. But I must not be too forward. I couldn't bear it if he thought I was—bothersome.*

She recalled often hearing her parents' rather formal "Good night, my dear" through the wall from their bedroom, even though they might not have spoken to each other during the evening, and she decided their rather meaningless gesture had some merit.

She cautiously put her icy hand on Abe's warm—if unconscious—flannel-clad arm, sighed deeply, and finally slept.

CHAPTER 3

THE NEXT MORNING they were on the road by daylight. The storm, like all their spring storms, had swept out over Lake Michigan. Susan checked the embroidered towel in her lunch basket. It was spread over a loaf of warm bread from the hotel kitchen. Sausages from home would complete their noon meal, and by night they should be at a German settlement on the north side of Chicago where Adolph lived. He operated a tailor's shop there, practicing a trade he had learned in Prussia.

Susan felt out of sorts. The days of anticipation, Abe's arrival, their wedding, and even their ride together were nearly over. Abe apparently was postponing intimacies Susan had nervously looked forward to. Her mother never spoke about the sexual part of married life. Nor did Olive. And the girls at boarding school had giggled and exchanged information— and what probably was misinformation—about things

26

married couples did. Susan was not sure how to tell true from false.

But she knew she must turn to practical plans now. The pleasant, easy part was almost over, and she began to think about dealing with old Adolph, with the dirty train, and with the trials of living with Olive, before she would have her own home. With her own kitchen. *And* her own bedroom. She trusted that there, Abe, who seemed reluctant even to touch her, would respond to her gentle affection.

Her dark mood passed. Now she was ready to try to draw her husband out and help him catch some of her growing ebullience.

Deep in his own thoughts, he was guiding the horse carefully over the icy early-morning road.

"Abe, do you know what I liked about you from the first, there at Olive's house?" She laughed. "You spoke to me in English. That man, I said to myself, is an educated man. How did I ever happen to find you out there in the wilds of Michigan?

"Is your new home going to be so wild then, Susan? It doesn't seem wild to me." Abe was watching her now, his face sober.

"But *you* grew up there. Mama says maybe your Mama and Papa and sister wouldn't have died if you had lived in a civilized place like Milwaukee. You know we probably couldn't have gotten a doctor in a hurry for Olive last summer if she'd needed one. I guess that's one reason it seems wild to me."

Abe was quiet for some time, and Susan was afraid she had hurt his feelings. She was learning, though, that he often mulled things over before he replied.

"Ma died when my sister Anna was born," he began. "But that was almost twenty years ago now, and I suppose we didn't have a doctor in our town then. And Pa was killed when a tree he was felling trapped his leg on the way down. I can still remember how I felt when I found him the next day. But it was too late by then to save him. I was six years old when that happened."

He paused again, this time for several minutes.

"And Anna—well, Anna got the consumption. And there's not a thing anybody can do about the consumption, whether it's in Michigan or in Milwaukee."

Susan was beginning to realize how much the memory of Anna meant to Abe. She knew he had always felt responsible for his sister, and that her death a year ago sent him into a period of depression he was only just beginning to recover from when she met him. A terrible, desolate look came over his face when he spoke about Anna.

But Susan tried again. "So where *did* you learn to speak good English? Everybody around there talks in Low Dutch most of the time."

"The folks around us say it's really Low German. It's a kind of easy way for ordinary German folk to talk to each other. Mr. Spencer settled on the next farm when he got back from the Great Civil War, and he took Anna and me in. We'd been living here and about. He couldn't speak much German, so I got so I talked it only at school. Of course we heard German in church. Good German.

"It was Mr. Spencer that sent us to the high

school." He turned to look at her, smiling broadly. "Do you know, that's why I wanted to marry you at first, too? When you started talking to me at your sister's, I said to myself, That's an educated woman. That's the kind of woman I'd like to have my family with."

"Have my family with" somehow eased a growing tension in Susan. Maybe Abe would soon stop acting like only a kindly brother. But now that he had given her a lead, she could not think of a tender reply.

She found herself saying only, "Papa insisted on English from all of us at home. He said if we were going to live in this country, we must speak the language of the men who run the government. Otherwise, he said, the government would run us."

"I wish I could talk more to your Pa. We might have something to say to each other."

Susan was surprised at her own bitterness when she replied, "You'd be the *first* person I ever saw who *could* have a conversation with him, then. He only talks. He never listens. Not to us girls, or to Mama, or even to Karl."

"He's a strong man, Susan. You will miss him."

Susan laughed. She forgot her homesickness of the night before. "The only person I will miss, Abe, is Laura. I guess I feel about her the same way you felt about your sister. She's so young—not even fourteen, you know—and she'll be alone with them now when the school term is over."

Susan opened her mouth to continue, but then she glanced at Abe and she closed it again. Mention of "your sister" had brought about a transformation of his face. It became the closed face of a stranger. She knew she must never treat the relationship between Abe and Anna lightly again.

So much I have to learn about living with this man, she mused. *Last summer when he was my beau, he never seemed to be hard to talk to*. There were always jokes and droll stories in the letters he had sent her during the winter.

She had a new thought. *Maybe he's as nervous and peckish as I am. Maybe men just react like this when they don't quite know what to do.*

This conclusion comforted her. *It will work out,* she told herself.

Susan looked with interest at the next couple they met, making their slippery way in a buggy on the ice crust of the road. The wife, her head wound in a dark scarf, appeared to be drained forever of emotion. Her eyes were dull and her mouth, a straight, bitter line over toothless gums.

Did those two communicate in a satisfactory way with each other? Had they shared secrets and dreams?

Did her own parents ever enjoy each other's company? No, she was sure they did not, at least they had not for many years past. Her mother, an old maid, and her father, a widower, had married and come to Milwaukee and set up housekeeping for the sole purpose of making a profit from selling land around the expanding city.

The children, Karl especially, were investments, too.

Susan watched Abe, now busy guiding their horse past a farm wagon that was lumbering through a great drift of snow blown across the road during the storm of the night before. The wagon carried branches fallen from trees along the road and harvested for a summer woodpile. The driver, a boy of fourteen or fifteen, with his face heading into a north wind, hardly looked their way. Already his farmer's eyes seemed hard and bitter.

Our marriage—and our family—will be different, Susan vowed.

CHAPTER 4

ADOLPH HELD A LAMP with a tall, clean chimney high above his head in order to see them better. He stood in the doorway of his home, a small box fitted into a row of neat frame houses all built under one roof, and peered out into the dark. His bald head shone in the warm light of the oil lamp.

Susan was glad to see him. After their last hours in the dirty, garbage-strewn outskirts of Chicago, Adolph's orderly German settlement gave her comfort, and stilled a new wave of homesickness. Milwaukee, the only large town she knew, had not prepared her for the open sewers and general filth and shoddiness of Chicago. Even the old man's querulous greeting did not spoil her arrival.

"Where you *kinder* been? You expect to keep me up all night?" He stepped out to examine the contents of the cutter. "You got my nice carved chest safe and sound?"

32

"Oh, Uncle Adolph, don't be cross," Susan cried. "We've had a long day."

Adolph grunted but said no more. He walked around the cutter again. "Looks like things are in pretty good shape," he growled. "You'd better take care of that horse, young feller. I'm liable to need her tomorrow to start back if it appears this weather won't hold. There's a stable down the block and around behind. Come in my kitchen way when you get done." He turned and started for the front door, holding his lamp before him. The snow continued to gleam in the cold world outside, and Abe started off.

"Mama has a list of supplies she wants you to buy for her, so I hope you can get them before you go back," Susan began, as she took off her hooded woolen cape and nestled up to Adolph's little round stove, thawing her frigid toes and fingers. "She's really counting on you." The neat horsehair sofa looked inviting, but she had been taught not to sit until asked.

"Bertha always did order everybody around. Anyhow, I can't get away without carting you and your luggage to the railway train, can I?"

Susan decided all her father's family must be alike. One time when she had attempted to discuss the subject with her mother, she had been told, firmly, "That's just their way. Don't be critical. They're good men, and their neighbors respect them."

Susan glanced around the room. Adolph kept a picture of his wife Martha on a small, highly polished table next to the sofa. Her father often said Martha's frown still made Adolph polish the furniture and floors, even though she had been in the graveyard for ten years. The room did look as neat as if a woman kept house. It smelled faintly of beeswax and of burning pine logs. Susan, though, longed for the privacy of what she knew would be a cold bedroom in order to tidy up. She could not bring herself to ask Adolph where she would sleep.

Then Abe came in, obviously in a good mood at the end of a tiring journey. He brought her carpetbag atop her uncle's precious chest, still wrapped in its protective quilt.

"Adolph!" Abe laughed, stretching his arms after carrying the heavy chest. He held out his hand. "You are a sight for sore eyes. If you'll just show Susan where you want us to sleep, I'll let her take our things in, and I'll warm up here by the fire. That's a trip I don't want to make again for a while." Susan stared at him as he carelessly sank to the horsehair sofa and then started to take off his dirty boots on the spotless rug.

And Adolph, fussy old Adolph, did not seem to mind at all. "Well, now, my boy." He smiled his tight little smile. "Make yourself at home while I tend to Susan." He picked up her carpetbag and a kerosene lamp from a small table by the door and led the way into his spare bedroom, which opened off the living room.

Susan, from the tiny, cold bedroom, heard the men making plans for morning. Wearily she drew a patchwork quilt that had been folded at the foot of the bed around her and leaned her head against a bedpost. To her dismay, tears sprang from her eyes and she began to weep quietly. Then she sobbed, first in great gasps that wrenched her body, and finally rhythmically, while she held onto the bedpost with both hands. At last she slowly calmed down to an occasional sniffle. *Whatever can be wrong with me?* she thought.

Wearily she drew the quilt around her again and started to sink onto the bed.

Susan suddenly became aware of the smell of fried potatoes and bacon coming from somewhere in the house. She knew Abe would soon come looking for her. Hurriedly she got up and splashed her face with icy water from a hand-painted china bowl. Examining her reflection in the mirror on the dresser, she saw no sign of puffy eyes or of red splotches on her pale face. She corrected the center part in her dark gold hair and pulled it back again into its severe bun. Then she folded the quilt neatly.

Susan realized the tensions that had been building for two days were gone. Humming a little tune—now she really felt like humming—she took up the lamp and opened the door to the warm living room.

Beyond it, inside his bright, spotless kitchen, Susan saw Adolph, busy with supper, and Abe, sitting at the table with a stein of beer. Abe was telling stories about their journey—stories that sounded funny the way he told them—and asking questions about Adolph's business and about Chicago.

In the morning when Susan looked out of her bedroom window she saw a world different from any she had ever envisioned. The sky was murky with a promise of rain, and a wild wind blew branches of trees and pieces of barrels and grimy shreds of cloth down the street. Even though there was still dirty snow piled in great heaps, swirls of dust towered above— and then swooped down on—pedestrians heading for work, or for a morning jug of milk, or hot breakfast bread from a bakery on the corner. A lone delivery cart, its driver's face muffled in a red scarf, braved the tempest.

Abe had already gone out to look after the horse, so Susan dressed quickly in the black serge suit she had bought to wear on the dirty train. She took her hooded cape with her to the kitchen, along with her carpetbag. Their trunk was by the door, ready to go into Adolph's buggy.

"I got to get you *kinder* to the station right away," declared Adolph for his morning greeting. "Sit yourself down and begin on those pancakes. I'll just pour you some coffee."

"Uncle Adolph, if you start back today, don't forget Mama's list. I really want to pick up some things myself, too, you know."

"No time! No time! I told Abe the same thing already. If that rain begins to come down, I won't get the cutter and your Papa's horse back before next Thanksgiving Day. *Then* the fur would fly!"

Susan poured herself a cup of coffee from the blue enameled coffeepot. The strong aroma filled the room. She watched Adolph, who was small and wiry like his brother, dash about the kitchen in the early-morning darkness, now tending the pancakes on the wood range, now peering through the gloom outside the window, now polishing his already shining table top.

She was eager to get on toward her new home, but she dreaded the train ride. Travelers brought them stories of train wrecks—thousands of passengers were killed and many more injured every year—and of the general filth and rowdiness.

"I expect this train will be a lot different from the kind I rode on last summer after I left the ferry, won't it, Uncle Adolph?"

"*Ja, ja*, it will, child. Those are good railway trains that run across the green countryside, with good passengers on them. But in this terrible city, well, I guess if I were you I'd just close my eyes good and tight—and my nose, too—until today is past."

"But Abe will be there. And Joseph and Olive came this way once. Abe will know what to do."

"A good deal of the time there's not a thing you *can* do. You'll see. You'll see."

A rush of wind and dust came in with Abe. "What a place to live!" He laughed. "Adolph, you'll have to come to visit us. You can store up some clean air and pretty sights before you have to get back to this dirty city."

"I'm not one for travel," Adolph grunted. "But you wait now, Susan, until you see the rest of Chicago. I live in the clean part of town. Just wait." He carefully set a china plate piled high with steaming pancakes at Abe's place at the table and motioned him with a sweep of his arm to sit down. Abe needed no further invitation.

Soon Adolph's horse Tom was picking his way through debris in the street and shaking his head to complain about the dust and smoke that thickened as they headed for the train station in the city. Delivery carts and buggies and hurrying people dressed in dark colors choked the bumpy, partially frozen alleys and streets. Puddles of filth drained off into dozens of greasy waterways, all of which would eventually arrive at the river. Tom put his ears back and snorted to show his displeasure.

"I don't usually take Tom down here," Adolph shouted to the others over the noise of horses and wagons and their drivers, and of the howling wind. "He sure lets me know how he feels about it. I wouldn't think of making Nellie do this job."

"Well, we're much obliged to you, Adolph," Abe shouted back. "It would have been a hard trip for Susan on the horsecar."

Suddenly Susan, with her first whiff of an overpowering, pungent, barnyard odor—rank even in the otherwise dreadful atmosphere—remembered Adolph's advice to hold her nose. She gasped and put her hand to her nose.

Adolph was anxiously watching a runaway team while he guided their buggy out of the stream of traffic, but the smell found him, too, and he chuckled. "That's only the stockyards!" he yelled. "They're way out across the city, but on days like this one, we've all got the stink in our back yards." He stopped Tom to let the runaway team pass, amid screams and shouts and a general clamor of wheels and hoofs.

"Fool driver! He could get everybody killed!"

Susan looked in vain for the smartly dressed Chicago matrons she had heard about. She decided they must wisely stay at home in such weather.

38

The rutted streets gave way to smoother, wider ones, and finally they reached the station. It was incredibly crowded there, but Susan sat in safety in the buggy while Abe bought their tickets.

"There's a train for the East that leaves in an hour," Abe shouted to them above the babble of voices and rumbling of carts when he came back. "I think we can find a seat right away. The passenger coaches are filling up already." He turned to Susan. "We won't travel in great style, I guess, Susan, but that's the way I came here."

"Well, *kinder*," Adolph shouted, "I pray you have a safe journey. That's mighty wild country you're going into, Susan. It's full of superstition and ignorance, you know."

Susan looked about her as Abe helped her from the buggy. "Uncle Adolph," she called back up to him, laughing, "it can't be much wilder than Chicago!"

But while Abe was getting their luggage Adolph seemed to be puzzling over a decision. At last he sighed and said, "Child, I think they stop stoking the stoves on the trains in March, and it must get mighty cold in those coaches. Here, you'd better take this." He lifted the fine red wool lap robe from his knees and handed it to Susan.

"I can use the one your Mama sent in the cutter to take me to Milwaukee, and then of course I'll get the railway train back."

"Oh, Uncle Adolph, I just couldn't! It's your best robe, isn't it?"

"It's meant for two people. You can see that. And then I haven't given you a wedding present, either,

39

you know. There, there, child. Let's not talk about it any more.''

He turned his horse's head and started out through the crowds, muttering to himself.

Susan's short, slender body was reasonably comfortable on the low wooden seats lining the walls of the coach, but Abe had to double his long legs and rest his arms on his knees.

After brushing away, as best she could, the cinders and dried apple peelings and cabbage leaves that covered even the cleanest areas, Susan wrapped Adolph's robe around both of them. There were seats much dirtier than theirs, with mud from boots everywhere.

The young woman next to Susan wore a black knit scarf wound around her head, and then around her neck. A boy of about four, bundled in sweaters and scarves, played at her feet with a couple of spools.

The woman was traveling alone, except for her child. Soon after the train jolted and ground out of the station, she started to cough, in violent spasms that racked her body. Susan wondered at times if she would get her breath.

Since they were packed closely together on the seat, Susan could feel the woman's agony, almost as if it were her own. In the clatter and confusion around them, the little boy continued to play, apparently unaware of his mother's illness—or unconcerned about it.

Susan laid her hand on the woman's arm. "Can't I get you some water?'' she shouted, indicating the big covered crock with a spigot, that stood next to the cold stove.

The woman straightened with an effort and looked at Susan. "It's all right now. Thank you kindly, though. It will pass. It's only consumption."

Just then a ragged boy of about twelve came into their coach with a basket of candy and sweet buns for sale. Susan felt as though she wanted to do something helpful for her seatmates, so she bought a penny candy for the child. She called to him, smiling and holding the green-and-white candy stick toward him.

For the first time the little boy raised his head from his play, and Susan was dismayed to see the same feverish face and sunken eyes she had noted in his mother. But the boy smiled shyly and took the candy stick, popping it into his mouth.

The woman seemed to be about to speak to Susan, but at once she was overcome by another fit of coughing. Out of the corner of her eye Susan saw the red-stained handkerchief that marked an advanced stage of consumption.

And she continued to cough, over the stocking cap of the little boy playing at her feet.

Susan crowded closer to Abe, looking at him to see whether he had noticed. He had.

He was staring straight ahead, with that desolate look of the day before closing himself away from her. He was, she knew, with Anna, watching her young life waste away in the same house—in the same bed—that would soon be Susan's.

41

CHAPTER 5

"I SUPPOSE MAMA AND PAPA really wanted us to stop in Chicago so Uncle Adolph could meet Abe. And Abe made Uncle Adolph laugh the whole evening," Susan told Olive when she recounted their adventures to her sister the morning after their arrival.

Misty, early March light was beginning to penetrate the corners of Olive's large, clean kitchen. Smells of breakfast cornbread laced with bacon still hung in the air.

"That was really the only good time we had all the way," she went on. "I don't think I'll ever get the dirt from that train out of my hair! It was such a relief to see Joseph sitting there in the buggy waiting for us when the train stopped."

She watched her sister as she kneaded bread dough. Olive had placed a breadboard on the blue-and-white checkered oilcloth that covered her square kitchen table in the center of the room.

People had always said that Susan and Olive looked alike, but Olive was growing quite plump, and worry lines were beginning to develop between her eyebrows. They still had the same white skin and the same fair hair they pulled severely back.

"Joseph says Abe's a man's man, Susan. He won't be much company for *you,* though, I'm afraid. You probably won't have a home like the one you're used to." Olive sighed. She seemed to sigh a lot more than she had the summer before.

Susan thought for a moment about the tense atmosphere of the household she had left. She answered Olive quietly, "It will be *my* home, too. I'll make it a place where we can have all the fun we both missed when we were growing up. You just watch me!"

Olive stopped to put more flour on her hands. She slapped the dough onto the breadboard.

"Mama wouldn't like to hear you criticize, Susan. And I'm afraid Joseph and I live the same way they do, even though we're way out here in Michigan with peasants all around us."

"Oh, Olive, do you really feel as though all your neighbors are peasants? Aren't there any folks from Prussia here?"

"Well, there's Reverend Schwenk. He speaks proper German, of course, and we sometimes have his family over for Sunday dinner. There are a few educated people in the village. But these farmers all come straight from Bavaria and the Saar, and I can hardly understand them. And they drink schnapps and chew tobacco and spit it on the floor like their fathers and grandfathers before them. If Mama ever comes out here, she will be shocked to see the children her grandsons will have to go to school with."

Susan slowly rocked the carved pine cradle as she chatted. It was good to see the baby again. He was fat and strong, like his brother Karl. Abe had talked about having a family. Surely their sons would be as promising as these two.

But almost a week had gone by, and she and her husband had not been together—except when they were both exhausted—with any privacy. "We're not animals, surely," was all Abe said when they were finally alone at Adolph's home. Then he kissed her on the cheek and turned to sleep, as quickly as he had in the hotel.

She longed for the time when they could be together in their own home.

Meanwhile there was work to do. The house they would live in was a half-mile away, across the fields. Susan wanted to visit it later in the morning. Abe was already there, checking on his cattle and horses and chickens. A neighbor had been caring for them.

Susan recalled Olive's telling her about Abe and his sister. Abe had rented the farm to make a home for Anna and himself after the first owner died, killed in a fall from a horse two years earlier. Then the house and barn and eighty acres of rolling farmland and woods were for sale, and Abe had put all his savings into a down payment.

Susan rose and began to stack the breakfast dishes. Then she poured hot water from a kettle into a dishpan and found a bar of lye soap. She worked at a small table near the stove.

"I'd never live in that house," Olive told her. With the bread dough rising behind the range, Olive had begun to churn butter. She opened the churn to add some salt. "Besides having had somebody die there just a little while ago—and in such an ugly way after that terrible accident—the house is only a barn, you know, a small barn. Patrick O'Neill moved it from across the road. It was built to be a barn over there, and it brought him bad luck in that place, too. It got hit by lightning, and some of the smoke from the burning hay smothered his horses."

"If it burned, how could he move it?" The dismal story depressed Susan.

"Oh, it was only the haymow, and the horse stalls below, that went. Then he and his hired man got the fire out. He built that part of the roof again and moved the whole barn across the road. And he lived in it. Mr. O'Neill was a rich man, but he lived like a poor one. He didn't even have a well near the house. Dug it down by his new barn. Of course he didn't have a wife to help him plan. Shanty Irish, that's what he was, for all his money."

"Have you visited there since Abe went to live in the house?" Susan asked.

"No, we weren't invited. None of the neighbors were. We all knew Abe's sister Anna was sick, but whenever I took a cake or some fresh bread to them, she always managed to come to the door. She never asked me in. She didn't take to her bed until the last."

"And *she* died there, too," Susan mused. "I'm glad I'm not superstitious. And I'm sure Abe's not, either. But it does give a person a turn, doesn't it?"

When she had dried the dishes and put them away, Susan knew she could wait no longer to see the house that would be her home. Susan thought about Olive's words as she climbed the rail fence back of Joseph's barn and began to cross the fields, soggy from a recent spring rain. The sky was bleak, the whole landscape utterly lifeless. A chill breeze swept across stubble from last year's corn crop and she pulled her shawl up over her head and wrapped it more closely around her body.

Susan wondered where the exact place that the horse had thrown Mr. O'Neill was. She would have to ask Abe. *I'm not going to worry about it, but I would like to know*, she thought. *Otherwise I'll see that accident behind every tree.*

Then Susan spotted Abe. He was drawing water for his horses from the well next to the new, unpainted barn. The barn-house, she noticed, needed paint, too.

But for a moment she almost forgot the figure at the well. She had a weird, fleeting impression that the forbidding, dark house lay crouching over there, waiting.

Susan took a deep breath and quickly turned around to Abe. He had seen her, too. She waved and called to him, "Come and meet me! Those horses don't need any more water!"

He put his bucket down, smiled, and waved back at her. Leaping the barnyard fence and starting toward her, he smiled again, that slow smile that sent shivers down her back. "I thought surely you'd be here an hour ago," he said. "Have I married a lazy wife?"

Today she must not fight. She was eager to see the

inside of the house that would, she hoped, be hers for the rest of her life. A coat of white paint on those streaked walls would make a world of difference in the impression it gave, Susan decided, ignoring that disquieting moment she'd had when she first saw it.

She must establish boundaries in her own home, in her relationship with Olive and Joseph, and in her relationship with Abe, too. Then she would feel secure.

Abe did not want to fight either, it seemed, and probably he was just teasing her to cover up his nervous concern over her first reaction to the home he provided.

"Susan," he said, "don't look too close right away. I've been doing some cleaning, and I've moved Anna's things to the attic, but my house sure doesn't look like Olive's, or like your Ma's, or even like Adolph's." He picked her up and swooped her over the rail fence, easing her carefully to the ground on the other side. "But I'm counting on you, you know. You won't let me down, will you?"

"First of all," she said, laughing, happy to see him close to the Abe she remembered from the summer before, "you have to stop saying 'my house.' It's *ours!*" She twirled around and around, letting her petticoats and wool skirt fly in the raw spring wind on her way up the path toward the barn-house. "Ours! Ours! Ours!" she cried.

Abe watched her, his confusion showing in his face. Finally he relaxed and began to follow her. "That's a new thought for me," he replied, with his smile beginning at the corners of his mouth and then lighting

47

up his eyes, "and the best one I've heard in a long time." He took her hand and led her around to the tiny front porch. It was made of pine planks on a stone base.

I can *make him do what I want him to,* thought Susan. *I* can *make a good home for him, and make him happy, too. My home* — our *home* — will *be different!*

Unexpectedly he picked her up again, this time to push the front door open with his boot and deposit her in her new living room. She looked around her. There was a worn, but clean, braided rug on the floor and two wooden rockers, hugging a potbellied stove.

One rocker was large and made of oak, and the other was smaller, a little beauty of carved pine, with a feather-filled blue cushion.

Abe's chair. And Anna's.

The stovepipe, which needed blacking, crossed the room so close to the ceiling there were scorch marks on the sun-faded, blue-flowered wallpaper. A sagging couch was in the corner on the far side, with a clean white cotton bedspread on it. A small walnut bookcase holding perhaps a dozen books stood against one wall. Frayed white gauze curtains, probably hung there by Patrick O'Neill's housekeeper, were on the two windows.

What could she say? Abe was watching her closely. Susan took a deep breath and turned to him.

"Abe, it's so *clean!*" she exclaimed. "Mama always says, 'Cleanliness next to godliness.' I hated to hear her say that when I had to scrub the sink over and over again, but I can see she had a point."

She searched his eyes. *Was it enough?* She went on, warming to her task enthusiastically, "And Abe, look at that empty corner. It will be just right for my piano, when Mama sends it along."

It was enough. Abe smiled. "Well, if this living room is going to have a piano, we'll need to do some fancying up first. I suppose you'll know how to do that."

Happily he crossed the room and opened the door to the kitchen. "Mr. O'Neill had a good cookstove. And the other furniture in here came with the house, too, so your kitchen will do, I guess. All you have to add to it is a woman's kind of talent."

A whiff of warm, rather stale air drifted from the kitchen. Abe had already built a fire in the wood range.

The plainness of the kitchen brightened for Susan, however, before a large package on the dark green oilcloth-covered table in the center. The package was wrapped in gold paper, and it had an artificial golden rose on the top. She was aware of Abe's eyes on her.

"Whatever is in that box?" she ventured. It shone in a stream of faint sunlight that had broken through the overcast sky. She turned to look at him. "Abe, you didn't forget after all!" she said.

"There wasn't any time until now we could be alone, Susan. Besides, I guess this is a wedding present for *both* of us. Open it up."

She unwrapped the gold paper carefully, saving it for some future special gift, and made a mental note to put the rose away in a box. Inside the wrappings was her wedding gift from Abe—a great family Bible,

49

fully ten inches thick and at least a foot and a half across, with an elaborately carved and gilt-decorated cover.

"It will teach our children ancient history," he told her, turning to sections filled with pictures of the world at the time of Moses. "And it will teach them morals," he continued, pointing out the Ten Commandments, again with vivid illustrations portraying each sin one should avoid.

"But the best part of our Bible is this." He smiled, opening the heavy book at its center. There, with curls of leaves and flowers surrounding blank spaces between lines, were places for family births, marriages, and deaths. And a central area to record names of many, many offspring.

Already at the top of the page he had written "Abraham Hesse" and "Susan Faust Hesse," with birthdates and their marriage date.

"Do you like my present?" Abe asked, obviously sure of her answer.

Susan paused before she replied. Had anything he had ever said to her sounded like what she wanted for them—companionship and, of course, love? She could recall only references to motherhood and housekeeping.

Susan looked up to see Abe's eyes, a little anxious now above his smile.

She *was* happy with the lovely Bible, and with the fact that he had bought it for her. She rushed to put her arms around his waist, under his woolen jacket, and to tell him so.

Abe held her close to him for a moment.

Then he took her hand and led her to the other door. It opened into the bedroom—Anna's bedroom. Abe had told her he continued to use his cot in the attic after his sister died.

But the room smelled clean and the walnut bed and dresser were free of dust. A neat white cotton spread covered the bed. Abe's hand gripped hers as he led her to the bed.

Abe was shy and awkward, and so was Susan. Only fleetingly did she think of Anna's lonely suffering in the same room. *Anna would have wanted her brother to make a good marriage,* Susan mused, as she lay back and looked briefly through what still seemed to be Anna's white window curtains. Then she smiled confidently as she met Abe's questioning eyes.

Susan and Abe spent the rest of the morning together in their house. She knew that in years to come she would date this day as the real beginning of their marriage.

CHAPTER 6

THEY WERE BOTH IN a happy mood as they started back for dinner with Olive and Joseph. "How will we explain a wasted morning? There's so much I have to do I shouldn't stop even for an hour," Abe wondered aloud when they reached the rail fence that marked the boundary of Joseph's orchard.

"We don't *have* to explain anything," Susan said. "I know I don't intend to."

"I've never been around people like Olive and Joseph. I sometimes feel guilty when I'm with them, even if I don't have any reason to."

"Now you know what my life has been like!" Susan laughed, and then she said, "But it's going to be different at *our* house." She turned her head to see Abe watching her.

"When you set your mouth like that, you do look like Olive, though," he said, grinning.

Susan frowned and formed a tart reply, but instead

she stopped to peer at a small, bent figure behind Joseph's barn. In the gloomy, misty air they had to walk up to the gate before they could tell it was Joseph. His woolen jacket had bits of straw sticking to the back and arms. His hat had come off and his bald head gleamed faintly with perspiration. Apparently he had just awakened and was being sick. A cider jug sat on the bed of the wagon he had planned to take to the fields after breakfast.

"I guess we weren't the only ones that wasted a morning," Susan whispered. "Now you surely won't feel guilty at Olive's table, will you?"

Abe looked grim. "Go on in the house," he ordered. "I'll throw some cold water on him and get him ready for dinner."

Only after Susan had marched herself around the barn toward Olive's porch did she realize she was behaving just the way she always did at home when her mother or father issued orders. Deliberately she slowed her steps. "Not that I would want to take care of a drunk," she muttered, "but I'd like to *decide* what I want to do."

Olive, in the nausea of another pregnancy, welcomed Susan's help with the babies, and with putting boiled potatoes and thick chunks of fragrant ham and a pot of steaming coffee on the table.

At the dinner table she held her head high, ignoring Joseph's sullen, weary face.

"How are you getting along then, Abe?" Olive asked, courteously, but without much interest. "Do you think you'll be ready to move in when Susan's storage trunk and piano come?" She watched him stick his fork into a large piece of potato and swirl it around in milk gravy. The fact that Olive's nostrils tightened as she watched was not lost on Susan.

"We got a lot done this morning," Abe lied, without glancing at Susan. "So I thought I'd help Joseph finish drawing that straw until time for chores. I can do my chores and then help him, if he needs me. Maybe this evening I could ride over to Gerber's place and see if their youngest boy would hire out to you for the summer. I hear he's ready to look for work."

He did not make a pretense of addressing Joseph, and Susan realized a transfer of authority was taking place.

Olive was not quite secure in her new role, though, so she replied, "Why, Joseph, that sounds like a good idea, don't you think? We'll need another man. That boy Fredrick should be a good worker like his brothers, and you could use a hired hand for chores, too."

She paused, waiting for a sign from Joseph. Finally there was a brief nod and a sigh. Then he returned to his dinner plate.

Susan stared at Olive, begging for a simple thank you for what Abe was doing for them. It was only after they had left the table that Olive said brusquely as she lifted the baby out of his highchair, "And we're much obliged to you, Abe." That was all.

Susan watched Joseph pull himself up from his chair and, hitching his suspenders slightly with his thumbs, head for the dining room couch. If there would be any straw brought into the barn that day, it would be Abe who drew it.

Then she heard the first spatter of rain. Leaving the dirty dishes on the table, she reached for her shawl from the coatrack and ran out to Abe, who was sitting in a white wooden rocking chair on the porch, puffing on a corncob pipe.

"Are you going to send me outside to smoke, too, the way Olive does?" He laughed, but she saw that he watched her closely for her reply.

"Oh, I don't know, Abe. Nobody ever smoked at our house. I hadn't even thought about it." She paused, a little confused. Then she went on, with more assurance, "Anyway, that's not what I want to talk about now. I've decided to spend the afternoon sorting out crocks and jars and linens Olive says she can spare, since I didn't have time to buy supplies in Chicago, and then I'll move out tomorrow morning. Early. If you can get Fredrick Gerber to help out here, I'll feel better about going, I guess, but whether you do or not, I'm leaving. I'll have some of my own linens coming with my trunk from Milwaukee."

Abe watched her quietly for a moment. "Can I move out with you?" he asked.

"Oh, Abe, don't make jokes," Susan cried. "Don't you see the way they treat you? And I can't stand that self-righteous face of Olive's—when her own husband is a drunkard!"

Abe smiled, knocking ashes from his pipe on the spotless porch railing. "Yes, but Joseph will be a 'von,' if his sick brother dies. Joseph von Braun. Olive will be pleased to put 'von' in front of her name. And then in front of the name of her oldest son, too. I can't offer our sons anything like that." He paused.

"People like your relations can drink all the hard cider they want to, but they can't destroy that—that *privilege* they've got."

Susan stopped herself from admonishing Abe about the ashes. Soon enough he would have to learn the niceties of civilized life. But she could not bring herself to respond to his bitter comments. He was right, but he was wrong, too, in the way he reacted. She decided to ignore the bitterness.

"While you go over to Gerbers'," she said, "I'll get my things together. Tomorrow morning we'll put them on a wagon and take them to our house."

Abe sat and rocked, watching the rain. His face was gloomy.

Susan's mood softened. "Oh, Abe," she implored, "don't you want to get into our own place as much as I do?"

He filled his pipe again. "Why do you have to take Olive's things? Anna and I got along with the linens and kitchen tools in my house." He paused, a glint in his eyes at last. "In *our* house. I kind of wish you wouldn't take anything from this house."

Susan wrapped her shawl around her shoulders more closely and sat down in the other wooden rocker. She began to rock slowly while her mind raced. She had not realized the extent of Abe's pride. But she felt she had to leave. Already her sister's house had become as oppressive as her parents'.

"I know you and Anna had a good life together," she finally said. "But I don't know how to live that way. It will be hard for me, and you'll have to help me. But I want to try. Now."

He looked at her with surprise. "A good life?" he asked. He knocked his ashes out to mingle with the rain on the railing and make streaks on the white floor beneath. "Well, then, Susan, I'm ready to move. You ride over to Gerbers' with me, and after that we'll go on into town and buy what you need to have until your own things come."

Susan was satisfied with their compromise. She went back into the house to wash the dishes and to tell Olive about their plans. But she wondered why Abe had been so startled when she mentioned his having had a good life with Anna.

Possibly he had not had a good life, not ever.

CHAPTER 7

THE NEXT DAY as she stood over a washtub, scrubbing sheets and towels on Anna's old galvanized washboard, Susan almost regretted her hasty decision. Heavy rain the day before had kept them from going into the village. If only she had waited until her own linen arrived from home, her first day in a strange house would have been easier. She noticed a break in the wooden rinse tub was letting water leak onto the worn linoleum of the kitchen floor. She probably should have done her washing outside.

"If I get these finished by noon, and the sun comes out for a while, we may be able to use the sheets by night," Susan told her sister.

Olive had walked over with baked beans for their dinner. "Imagine Mama hanging a washing out at noon!" she scolded. "Her white clothes are on the line every Monday morning by eight. I try to keep the house the same way." She paused. "You can always send Abe over for some of our bedding after supper, if you have to, you know.''

Susan ignored her offer, concentrating on running the sheets through an old wringer, while Olive inspected the mostly empty cupboards and then climbed the stairs to the unfinished attic. Susan heard her moving Abe's cot up there in the far corner. She came down as Susan was going out the back door with a basket of soggy clothes.

They hung the towels and sheets together in silence. Little Karl played with a wooden spoon, digging into some wet soil under the clothesline. When they had finished, Olive said, ''Well, it's time I got home and woke the baby up. Don't try to do too much the first day, child.''

''Thank you for your help, and for the food,'' Susan responded quietly.

As Olive took Karl's chubby hand and started back toward the field, a misty sun broke through the rain clouds. Olive turned around, surveying the square, barnlike house.

''It's a good, strong house, Susan,'' she said. ''Not like a log cabin, that lets in wind and snow during the winter.'' She warmed to her subject. ''The first thing Abe must do for you is to build a nice porch. Then there will have to be a cistern dug under the house and connected to a pump for soft water. There's a respectable cellar, but you need a fruit cellar, too, like ours. All proper farmhouses have fruit cellars. After that, he'll have to finish the attic. There's plenty of space for three nice rooms. Those three big rooms downstairs are all right for the two of you, but you must make plans for the future. Keep these things in mind, Susan. Don't let up for one instant until you have them!''

Susan stared at her for a moment. Then she began to laugh. She laughed until the tears rolled.

''Olive,'' she gasped, wiping her eyes on the corner of her apron, ''I'm so glad you came!''

Olive cried, ''Susan! Stop! Whatever has come over you?''

''Oh, Olive,'' Susan finally managed, ''look! You've brought the sun!''

Long after Olive, with a worried expression, had climbed the barnyard fence to cross the fields, Susan sat in the sunlight on her pine-board porch and dreamed. She dreamed of fruit trees in the yard, of flowers, of children playing among the trees and flowers, and of cisterns and fruit cellars and pumps and finished attics, but most of all, of her own priority—a well next to the house.

She finally rose to take her bucket to the well at the barn for more water, this time for cleaning cupboards and floors. Abe, coming in to dinner a few minutes later, found her singing to herself while she scrubbed the kitchen floor in the sunshine.

''Say, now, where's my dinner?'' he called through the door. ''Now that the rain's over, and the frost is out of the ground, I can begin my plowing. I want to put in a good afternoon.''

Susan stopped and looked at him. ''*Our* dinner is in the oven. Olive brought it. I hope you don't mind.'' She began to smile and then she cried, ''Oh, no! Don't come in like that—with your muddy boots. Besides,

60

the floor's wet. Come outside with me and rest on the porch, until the floor's dry. I'll spread a quilt on that gravel over there and we'll have a picnic in the sun for our first dinner together.''

Abe seemed torn between duty and pleasure—pleasure in doing what Susan wanted. "Oh, well," he grumbled, "all right, but it seems like a pretty fool thing for a farmer to have a picnic on a working day." He backed out of the door and began to wipe his boots carefully on some new grass.

"I'm glad you didn't wonder what the neighbors would say if one passed by," Susan called, gathering a ragged quilt, the pot of beans, and some of Olive's freshly baked bread. "You can run down to the well for a bucket of water for us, Abe, if you care to." She might as well start laying the groundwork for her first request—a well close to the house.

Susan placed tin cups and a pot of butter and some knives and forks on the quilt she had spread in the sun. Returning with the water, Abe asked, "Where did you get that way of talking, that 'if you care to'? It seems to me it still doesn't give me much choice, even though you don't snap out orders like 'Get the water!' "

He sat down and started to fill one cup with steaming beans laced with crisp chunks of pork. Another he filled with water. Without waiting for Susan, he began shoveling food into his mouth.

Susan watched him, shaking her head. But she would not lose her happy mood. "Imagine Mama, letting me have a picnic at home on an ordinary work day!" she said.

Abe looked up. "At home?" he asked. "Susan, *this* is your home."

Susan fell silent. He did not seem hurt, but spoke as though he were only stating a fact.

Finally she replied. "No, Abe, you're wrong, too. It's *our* home."

Directly after their dinner, Abe filled a jug of water at the well. He took the jug and some bread to the field with him. He planned to work until dark, so Susan had a long afternoon to finish her cleaning. For supper she planned to cook a pot of potatoes, carrots, onions, and cabbage, along with a strip of ham. Abe's cellar still held enough winter-stored food to supply their table until garden crops would come along. She found a crock of pickles and one of sauerkraut, and barrels of beans and dried corn. When she went out to feed the chickens and gather eggs, she saw the remains of Abe's garden and knew there must be parsnips and horseradish ready to dig. She was eager to start house-keeping in earnest.

When darkness began to close in, Susan lighted a lamp and set out tin plates on the cracked green oilcloth that covered the table. In the future, she decided, she would always meet Abe when he returned from the field in the evening and walk back to the barn with him, but tonight she was tired. She sat down at the table and took her new Bible out of its box. A strong wind began to rise. She knew Abe would have to stop his plowing before long. He would stay in the field as late as he could, though, for the east wind promised more rain.

"This Michigan weather is terribly depressing," Olive had told her. "We almost never have sunshine two days in a row. Everybody is sick in the spring, and old folks do well to last out the damp and cold."

Susan hoped Abe would be content with his day's work and happy to be with her again at night. She looked forward to his reading stories from the Bible while she washed dishes. *We must begin by sharing everything we can,* she thought.

The first section of the great book described the ancient world the Israelites knew, and Susan soon became engrossed in a fascinating account—with vivid illustrations—of Egyptian burial customs. When she finally looked up, the dark made her feel chilled and a little uneasy. She rose to get her shawl and to put a stick of wood from the wood box by the door into the range.

Then, as she lifted the lid from her pot of simmering, fragrant vegetables, she heard a sound. It seemed to come from somewhere in the house. She could not tell what *kind* of sound it was, though she strained her ears to hear it again.

"Surely Abe doesn't have rats. I haven't found any sign of them anywhere. Could a squirrel have come in while I was in the yard taking down clothes or out tending to the chickens?" Susan realized she was mumbling audibly.

She went to the window and peered out, but the shadowy darkness showed no sign of Abe and the horse, coming toward the barn. She sighed, wrapping her wool shawl more closely around her shoulders, and sat down again, trying to concentrate on the pictures of mummies and pyramids that had seemed so compelling a little earlier.

Then she heard it again. This time it was clearer. There was a short cry, a pause, and after that a low moan. Susan gasped, putting her hand to her mouth. She had not realized how tense she had become. Her first impulse was to run outside and find Abe.

But she had never been in the fields around their house at night. And even though she had never been alone in a strange house, either—moreover, a house with such a reputation for calamity—she preferred its island of safety to the possible dangers lurking outside in the dark.

This is my first night here, she said to herself. *If I can't stand on my own feet now, I never will.* A comforting thought arose. *What would Mama do? She would take that lamp and hunt that sound out.*

Susan picked up the lamp and grasped it firmly in one hand. With the other, she opened the door to the bedroom, holding her lamp so that light could chase the shadows back behind the bed and into the corners. There was no sign of movement. But as she stood there she heard the cry again.

Susan jumped slightly, unconsciously waiting for the moan, which followed just as it had before.

The sounds now seemed to come from the closed-off living room.

Before she could become too frightened to do so, she ran to the living room and threw the door open. Again she could see no rat or squirrel in the corners when she raised the lamp high above her head. There was no evidence of anything's having been disturbed

64

since she had finished cleaning there in the afternoon.

But then her eyes fastened on the smaller of the two rockers—Anna's rocker. The little carved rocker with its blue cotton cushion was moving slightly, not as though the wind were blowing through the room and causing it to stir, but rhythmically, as though a body were in it. There was a faint sound of a floorboard's creaking beneath the chair.

"It's not true," Susan said to the empty room. "These things are not true. They do not happen." Her eyes grew dry from staring, and she blinked them.

When she opened them, the rocker had stopped.

A great gust of wind blew past her from behind and she whirled, with the lamp still held high, to find Abe standing in the kitchen door.

"Well, and what are you lighting the whole house for, Susan?" he asked, laughing. He looked closer. "Is there something wrong? You aren't upset, are you? I didn't mean to be so late, but I wanted to work as long as I could see. It doesn't seem so dark out there when your eyes are used to it, you know."

He took off his boots and set them by the door. Then he poured water from a pail on a bench set against the wall into a washbasin and began to scrub his hands and face.

Susan could not talk about what had happened now, while it was fresh. As long as Abe believed her pallor came from concern for him, she would let him think so. She took a deep breath, closed the living room door without looking back, and geared herself up to setting their supper on the table. Her hands shook as she poured coffee into their tin cups.

Abe was obviously happy with his afternoon's work, and as soon as he had finished his first helping he started to talk, in the easy way he had chatted at Adolph's home after their exhausting day in the cutter.

"Susan," he began, "did I ever tell you this house is haunted? I've never seen any spooks here myself, though—mostly, I guess, because my mind doesn't run in that particular direction."

Susan felt her face grow pale again. But he did not notice because he was dishing up another plate of vegetables and ham. She tried to keep her voice even. "What makes people think it's haunted?"

"Well, first there was Mr. O'Neill's housekeeper. She said she couldn't stay here, even after they dug the body up and sent it away."

"The body? Oh, Abe, what are you talking about?"

He did not look her way but continued to shovel his food into his mouth. All at once his usual slow response infuriated her.

"Look at me!" she cried. "Raise your eyes and look at me! You're making a joke, aren't you!"

He looked up, a grin spreading across his face. "Susan, I swear to you, it's true. O'Neill was killed when his horse threw him, you know. And it was winter then. The ground was frozen and the roads were all snowed shut with a blizzard that lasted for a good five days.

"The housekeeper called in some folks that lived on the road where Olive and Joseph live, and they decided to bury him down in the cellar. It was about a week before they could get his relations here and have the funeral."

Because Abe told the story as though it were a kind of gruesome joke, Susan managed a smile. "And she thought the house was haunted after that? I'm not surprised." She paused. "What kind of noise did the ghost make?"

"I never did find out." He grinned. "But they do say you can hear a horse's whinny on the road down to the woods on winter nights, when there aren't any horses out." He was enjoying himself.

Susan drew a long breath. "I'm glad," she said, "that *you* haven't heard or seen anything. Besides, Mr. O'Neill's Irish housekeeper was probably as superstitious as they come."

Abe sat back and lit his corncob pipe. "Well, I must say I have to agree with you."

Then the desolate look Susan was beginning to recognize came over his face. "But, you know, Anna thought the house was haunted, too. She didn't even want neighbors to come in for fear whatever it was might scare them. She could live with the spook, she said, but she was afraid folks would think she was an odd one if she talked about it. I finally decided it must be the fever that made her act that way. Fever can do things like that to people, don't you think?"

Susan rose to clear the dishes away. "Of course you're right," she agreed, as she poured hot water from a kettle on the stove into a dishpan. "There's always an explanation. There always is."

She put the cry and the moan and the rocking chair into the remotest corner of her mind and, for the moment, she left them there.

After supper Abe took a straw from his pocket and

67

lit his pipe again from the glowing end of a stick of wood in the dying fire in the range. Then he brought out the great Bible and laid it out on the green oilcloth where Susan had carefully washed and dried a clean place.

She poured hot water from the teakettle into a rinse pan across the table from him and watched him with affection while he read in the light of the oil lamp, his finger following each word, the way a child would read.

"I'll start with the New Testament, Susan," he said, "and we'll read a chapter every night." He peered up at her through the lamp's warm glow. "Our children will hear a chapter every night, too."

"And even our grandchildren?" She smiled back at him.

The door behind her to the cold, dark living room was closed, and Abe's warm presence and the comforting words he was reading helped her swallow the panic that rose whenever she remembered how frightened she had been.

Long after Abe had fallen asleep Susan found herself listening tensely—for cries or moans, or even a softly rocking chair. There was no sound, though, beyond the hooting of an owl and the steady patter of spring rain echoing through their empty loft.

CHAPTER 8

THE NEXT MORNING'S weak sunshine called Abe back
to his plowing. The mountains of unaccustomed
chores Susan faced formed a pattern for their day, and
for the days to come. Susan had never known a house
like this one.

I surely can't complain to Abe, she told herself
when she carried yet another bucket of water from that
far well, *and I won't say anything to Olive. She would
only write to Mama, and then Mama would lecture me
about German peasants.* Again she shoved to the back
of her mind the memory of Anna's chair, of those
disturbing sounds, and of Abe's mysterious, dark
looks whenever he thought about his sister.

*And if I wrote her about the chair, she'd say maybe
Karl was right about superstitious, ignorant people
from Bavaria.*

She put her hands on her hips. "You're not going to
beat me, House, you know," she declared aloud.

"I'm not a superstitious, Low Dutch peasant. People with some education and some good religious training don't believe in ghosts. You don't scare Abe, and you're not going to scare *me,* either!"

The house looked a little forbidding in the misty light. It took a firm resolve to make Susan pick up the bucket and enter the kitchen again.

"The first thing I'm going to do when I get settled will be to paper these walls with some bright colors," she continued, chattering on aloud to the gray wallpaper and green oilcloth. "Then when Mama asks what I want for my birthday I'll have her send me some yellow cotton cloth, and I'll make yellow curtains for the windows. After that, even in the winter my kitchen will be cheerful."

Susan took a deep breath and threw open the door to the living room. "And I won't shut this room off. When my piano comes and I get some nice embroidered glass curtains, if that crazy chair," she stated defiantly, staring at the small, still rocker, "wants to rock, why, it will have to rock for everybody to see!" She sang loudly while she rolled up the sleeves of her calico shirtwaist and began to wash the windows.

All morning long the chair did not move.

That evening as soon as it started to get dark, Susan wrapped her shawl about her and walked down past the barn and into the lane that led to the pasture and to the field of rich, dark clay Abe was plowing. Faint smells of turned earth and of cows in the next field were wafted on a light breeze. The low, red glow in the west promised a fine sunrise. Their dog was not used to her yet, and he spent the days in the fields with Abe, but as soon as he saw her coming, he leapt the rail fence to go to find the cows in the pasture and round them up. He seemed to know the workday was over.

Susan was waiting for Abe when he came to the end of the row. "You've really trained Bennie, haven't you? I've never milked cows, but I suppose I could. Wouldn't it help if I milked the cows for you?"

Abe was amused. He took off his old felt hat and wiped his forehead on his sleeve. "They wouldn't give you any milk, Susan. A fine farmhand you'd make!"

A sharp remark was pushing past her lips when she saw how tired he looked. She bit her words back, but she resolved to teach him he must not taunt her. *She* had been working hard all day, too.

"Then you'll have to show me how to milk a cow," she managed.

He looked at her, searching her face for a moment. He paused after that to take a fresh bit of chewing tobacco from a package in his wool jacket. Susan turned her head so she would not have to watch him. He did not chew tobacco in the house, and he probably knew she would not want him to. It pained her even to see him tuck the cud into his cheek and spit the juice expertly at a nearby fence post. She wrinkled her nose at the strong, sweet odor.

"Susan," he finally said, "I'm glad you don't know how to milk a cow. I won't have you around the barn or in the fields, either. If I'm not able to get the work done, it just won't *get* done."

71

"But can't I help you at all? I thought farm women worked right alongside the men. I know some of the women I met last summer do."

"I suppose you could help Bennie bring the cows up to the barn at night for me. I'd be much obliged if you did that."

Susan was glad she had refrained from answering his teasing remark. She recalled Olive's calling him a "man's man." But he *was* going to be good to her, as she had known he would. She hoped she could train him to be a little more refined, too.

"Besides," Abe went on, "before long you'll be too busy raising a family to have any time outside the house." He smiled at her through the fading light.

This time she could not resist answering back. "Oh, Abe, let's take a year or two to get the house ready and to get to know each other. We don't need to have all that responsibility right away."

He peered closely at her. "Whatever are you saying?" He paused, apparently looking for the right words. "You know, a home, for me, means children. I've always seen other families with a father and mother and children, and it seems like the right way for people to live. I don't even remember a life like that. Besides," he continued, setting his jaw, "whatever is God's will is the right way, don't you think?"

Visions of those lines with the scrolls and leaves decorating them in the big Bible swept through her brain.

"Of course, Abe," she replied, "but we have minds of our own, too. It's going to take quite a while for you and me to learn to live together." She watched

72

him unhook the plow and turn the horse toward the barn. "We really are awfully different."

"Most husbands and wives are. Just look at Olive and Joseph."

"But surely we're not going to live the way they do, either." She made a wry face. Then she went on. "I'd like to have us go ahead being separate people. You can do things you want to do sometimes. And I like music and I like sewing, too, you know. And then we'll do things together, of course."

Abe stopped to open a gate. He watched Bennie take the cows through the opening into the lane. Finally he closed the gate after Susan before he spoke. "Well, that's a new one for me. It seems to me there's a lot you have to learn about the hard work of farming." He chuckled. "Did you get some of your ideas from that fancy school you went to back in Milwaukee? I'll bet those ladies never saw a hoe!"

Susan bit her tongue to keep from answering. She was hurt and a little angry that she had to spell out an arrangement that was clear in her parents' marriage, unsatisfactory as the marriage seemed to her in other ways. *But then,* she thought, *maybe it took them quite a while to reach that understanding.*

At length she trailed along behind Abe in the darkness, making more plans and humming to herself.

CHAPTER 9

THE NEXT DAY Susan began to plan a proper welcome for her piano. Even though she was afraid Abe might not want her to, she accepted five rolls of wallpaper Olive offered, paper that displayed roses among soft green, trailing vines.

"I had picked out these roses for the parlor," Olive said with a sigh. "But Joseph wanted a quiet, gray room for our mohair furniture. I'd already cut into one roll when he told me to get something else, but I'm sure five will be enough for that little living room of yours. I really can't use it anywhere else myself."

"Well, I'm glad to have it. So now before I need to start the garden, I can decorate the room for my piano."

"When you get up enough gumption to make Abe build onto that barn you live in, you'll have a parlor, too, and you can put your piano in there."

Susan smiled to herself. Olive could never give

anything without a remark or two that spoiled it all a little.

"If you'd like me to, you know I'd be glad to keep your piano here in my parlor for a few years until you have a nicer place for it," her sister continued.

That was too much! "Olive," she cried, "that piano is *mine!* Even if I lived in a stable—or in rented rooms in one of those awful shacks we saw in Chicago —I would have it with *me!*"

Olive watched her as she strove to hold back the tears. "There, there, child," she said. "It's no use getting upset." She looked at her closely. "Is everything all right over there at your house?"

"Everything's fine," Susan declared, stooping to pick up the rolls of paper and the brush Olive had loaned her. "I'll try to get the strips measured and cut this afternoon." She determined to say nothing more that would start an argument.

"Well, I'll make paste tonight and be over early tomorrow afternoon to help you get started." As Susan was opening her mouth to decline further offers of help, Olive surprised her with, "You don't know how good it is to have you here, child."

Somehow the walk back across the fields was easier than her walk over, and she rehearsed what she would say to Abe about accepting the wallpaper. Maybe in the kitchen she would just take the old gray paper off and put light green paint on her walls. She would be able to buy paint from the lumberyard in the village.

"There are things a woman has to make decisions about," she declared to herself. "I wouldn't advise Abe about buying a harness."

As soon as she got inside the house, she looked over the furniture in the living room. "Maybe if we had more chairs, I could persuade Abe to move that little rocker out," she thought. It was too early now, though, to disturb a chair that probably meant a great deal to Abe, because it had been Anna's, and obviously only Anna's, when they had lived there together.

She had the chairs moved back against the wall and her rolls of paper spread out on the living room floor when Abe came in at noon for dinner. While she was taking boiled potatoes off the stove, he looked through the now always-open door and saw what she had been doing.

"What's this?" he thundered.

Susan looked at him in astonishment. She took a quick breath. "Is something wrong?" she asked.

"Where did you get this wallpaper?" he demanded.

"Olive—" she started to answer.

"How long are we going to go on playing poor relations? *I'll* buy our wallpaper. I want you to take that back this afternoon. Mind, now, Susan, I want that to go back!"

Susan felt her face grow pale, but she stood her ground.

"This paper came from Chicago, and it would take a month before I could get some like it, even if we could afford it," she said. She tried another approach. "Oh, Abe," she said, "I'd never realized how lonesome Olive is, and how much she likes having me here, and how much she really wants to do things for us."

Abe grunted. "Maybe I can't make you understand.'' His temper, which Susan had not seen before, seemed to subside a little while he began to fill his plate with potatoes and bacon. She waited, watching him quietly. He said nothing more, and she sat down. Abe said a brief prayer and they started to eat.

Finally he pushed his plate back. ''All my life, since I grew up,'' he began, ''I have not owed anybody for anything. When a man takes something from somebody, he owes a debt. And I don't want to owe Joseph anything—especially Joseph.''

''But, Abe, relatives always owe each other things. Did you feel that way about staying with Uncle Adolph?''

''No, I guess not. But then, Adolph's different. If he came here he could stay with us, too. Anyway, Adolph wouldn't throw it up to us that we owe him anything. Joseph's rich, and he acts rich, too, on top of it all.''

''You helped *him,* you know. You took care of him when he was drunk, and you got a boy to put his crops in and help him in the barns.''

''Don't think I haven't mulled that one over while I've been plowing these last few days. The worst thing I could do for him was to take care of him when he was in such a state. Most men would probably be able to laugh it off. But Joseph's proud, you know, and he thinks he has to keep up appearances in the neighborhood.'' He paused. ''We'll never get along, Susan. We'll never get along.''

She saw the sorry logic of his words. ''But,'' she ventured, ''Olive isn't that way. She really wants to help us—for all her sharp tongue.''

77

She paused, seeing Olive in a new light. "You know, Abe, I almost feel sorry for her, with all her money, yet such a sad home life. Don't be mad at me, Abe. She wanted to help me. She wanted to give me the paper, and she wants to come and help me put it up. Maybe just to get herself out of that house."

He looked at her silently for a moment. Then he chuckled a little and reached for his walnut cake. "I was pretty noisy there for a while, wasn't I? I haven't been around women very much, except for Anna. And Anna was always sick when she lived here with me."

"So you bossed her around, and she let you do it."

The implied criticism of Anna brought a quick rejoinder. There was anger in his voice. "No, Susan, it wasn't that way. Anna didn't let me boss her, but she did let me take care of her, and I guess I did all the deciding for her, too." He sighed. "That's the way it was."

He did not sound angry now.

Susan grinned. "Well, you won't have to make decisions any more, at least not all of them."

Abe smiled, too. "I can see that." Then his smile faded. "Every time I look at that wallpaper, though, I'll remember it was Joseph's money that bought it."

So things were settled, Susan thought, but not really in a way she would have liked.

"Susan," Abe said after he finished eating his ham and eggs the next morning, "maybe we should take a little walk." He had been up even earlier than usual to finish his chores before breakfast in order to get back to the field.

78

Susan turned from the dishpan she was filling with hot water. "Now?" she asked. "At seven in the morning?"

Abe kept his eyes on his hands, fingers tightly folded, on the table in front of him. "I was awake a lot, Susan, after we talked," he said. "Maybe I should explain a few things to you. I guess it's best to show you, too, though."

He rose with a sigh. At the door he turned and smiled slightly, although his eyes looked tired and gloomy.

"Come along now," he said. Bennie, on the porch, rose to go with them.

Susan left the dishes and followed him through the door, wrapping her black wool shawl around her shoulders.

Abe headed toward the mist rising from the swampy land surrounding the woods. He did not wait for her when she stood, puzzled, in the driveway. He seemed so deep in thought he obviously did not realize she was not alongside him.

Finally, with a little laugh, Susan called, "Where *are* we going? Wait for me!" and ran to his side. Abe was walking with his hands held tightly together in front of him. She put her arm through his. At once, he closed one hand over hers.

Suddenly she felt very close to him, closer than she ever had before.

Neither spoke while they walked through the mist. In the woods oak and elm and walnut trees rose high on either side, almost shutting out the early light. There was no wind, and no sound except for an occasional bird's song. Bennie trotted on ahead, his perked-up ears searching for sounds from the swampy woods.

Susan had not walked down this back road before. Olive's home and the main road to the village lay in the other direction.

Beyond the woods began hilly land she had seen in the distance the summer before. It was there, Abe told her, he had been born. After a few moments the narrow road led them to the ruins of a log cabin. The roof had a hole in it. Part of the stone chimney was crumbling. One could see through cracks between the logs. And behind the cabin only a fire-blackened stone foundation showed where a barn had stood.

Abe stopped in the road. "Here's where Anna and I grew up," he said. "At least until I was six years old. Anna was three when that tree killed Pa."

He did not look at Susan. His face was withdrawn. "Pa was renting this place from Mr. Spencer's pa. The old man died while his son was away fighting in the Great Civil War. And just after Pa died, lightning took the barn."

Abe started walking toward a small orchard of apple and cherry trees growing next to the far side of the cabin. His hand was no longer on Susan's.

But she clung to him, fearing what he would show her next.

They stopped at a spreading russet apple tree. Beneath it were three small, white tombstones. The two older ones were tipped toward the sunken clay soil. The third tombstone was new. A stalk from a field rosebush stood in front of it.

"Pa wanted Ma close by," Abe said. "Not off in a graveyard. So Mr. Spencer let me put Pa here, too. When I grew up I paid Mr. Spencer for this little piece of orchard." He was silent for a moment. "Then last year," he went on, "I put Anna with them."

His voice was tense, but controlled. "Susan," he said, "except for me—and you—there's nobody named Hesse around here any more."

Susan could find no words. Tears ran down her cheeks, tears for the little boy and his sister. And for the young man who finally lost Anna, too.

She took his hand and held it to her cheek.

He stood quietly, as though he were alone. He did not respond to her.

CHAPTER 10

SUSAN WASHED THE DISHES. Then she punched down the bread dough for a second rise and set the bread pans on a wobbly wooden bench behind the wood range. Not once did she glance into the living room.

She hummed to herself. After a while she began to vocalize and finally she even sang a few lines from a Handel oratorio. Loudly. Defiantly.

Now I know I'll have to send our children back to Milwaukee for their education, she decided. For the first time Susan realized she was seeing her new neighborhood through Olive's critical eyes—something she had vowed never to do.

Immediately she understood she must begin to fight her own growing disillusionment with Abe's world. *Abe and our children,* she told herself, *are going to have a richer life than the kind those three poor souls in their pitiful little graves endured in this dreary land.*

And it will be up to me to help provide it. That's why

Abe married me. Because he wanted an educated woman to have his family with, he said. She took a deep breath. *I sometimes wonder if he has any notion of the kind of caring a wife really needs, though.*

The fog had lifted when Susan took two buckets to the well for more water. She sat for a few minutes on the stone wall circling the well, and pulled her shawl up over her head. A chill wind was rising and the sun had disappeared behind scudding clouds.

The square house looked grim and forbidding. A twisted walnut tree near the kitchen door and a giant elm in the front yard dwarfed its graying board walls.

It could use a few spreading bushes and a lot of bright flowers, Susan mused. *And of course some paint. First some paint. As soon as Abe is finished harvesting, I'll help him paint.*

Her vision blurred and she fantasized for a moment the tiny log cabin Abe had showed her after breakfast. She had not seen the Spencer house where he and Anna grew up, but they might well have found their barn-house quite luxurious in comparison with that crumbling hut just beyond the woods.

Susan knew she could never risk hurting Abe by being critical of their house, or of anything else he provided. He *was* kind, and he was, as her mother described her Uncle Adolph, a good man.

And when he felt happy, the slow searching smile that lighted his face sent her flying to him. Abe always hugged her back, too, affectionately. But not with anything more than affection.

She felt a slight chill when she remembered the way he had withdrawn from her beside Anna's grave.

83

Susan took up the buckets and started toward the kitchen. On the way she hit upon a plan that might solve one of her problems. She decided to confront the problem right away.

Once inside the house, she threw her shawl over a chair and walked with firm steps into the living room. She sat on the sagging couch, now covered with Adolph's red carriage robe, straightened her back, and folded her hands tightly in her lap.

Susan's new compassion for Anna helped to dispel the uneasiness she had often felt when she was alone in the living room. She still did not believe in anything other than a rational reason for the strange rhythmic movement of the little carved rocker.

But she did not sit in Abe's chair. Somehow sitting in his chair would make her a companion to whatever it was that seemed to visit the pine rocker and start those floorboards beneath it creaking. She sat on the couch—a guest, not a companion; not a believer.

It was dim in the little room. The worn, white muslin curtains screened sunlight already filtered through black clouds. Wind in the branches of the great elm outside patterned an irregular changing of light on the windows and created an illusion of movement inside.

Susan laughed in relief. Her clenched fingers relaxed. That's all it was, she thought. An illusion. On a day like this one could imagine almost any kind of movement when the wind blew and light patterns changed. The same thing might have happened when her lamp had flickered over the room on that first night.

"Anyway," Susan found herself addressing the little chair, "I want you to know I feel sorry for you. I feel sad about your sickness and your loneliness.

"But that's all over now. Don't try to come here to be near Abe any more. I'm taking care of him, and I always will."

Susan stopped abruptly, feeling a little foolish. She laughed again, this time nervously. The room had come alive with shadows and light and the sound of creaking rafters. The wind blew erratically, now gusting, now dying away to a murmur.

All at once she found herself listening tensely for the moans she had heard that first night. But there were no moans.

Susan knew she could sit on the couch no longer. *It's just nerves*, she thought. *I've never been alone like this all the time before*. She got up and stared hard at the rocking chair. "Anyway," she said aloud again—because the sound of her voice gave her courage—"when my piano comes and it takes up a lot of space in here, nobody will even notice a little rocker like that. Even Abe won't notice it. Anna's rocker won't be important to him any more."

Standing in the doorway to the kitchen, Susan looked back over the room once more. Her living room. No one else's. She took a deep breath. She must finish her work. Olive would be here soon.

Well, that's settled, she told herself.

Then as she turned toward the kitchen to get back to the water buckets, still sitting inside the door where she had left them what seemed like an eternity before, she stopped sharply. The floorboards behind her were beginning to creak.

CHAPTER 11

A WEEK LATER Olive came over with news that Susan's piano would be at the train station in two days. Joseph had gone to the village and come back with a letter for her from Milwaukee. Susan's father had helped take the piano to the train himself.

"I recalled again, as I watched the men load the piano onto the cart, how pleased you were with your twelfth birthday present," her mother wrote in anticipation of the delivery, "and how much we always enjoyed hearing you play hymns on Sunday evenings."

"Mama never talked about enjoying my playing before," she told Olive, with a sad smile. "She only told me about the notes I missed."

"Go on with the letter," said her sister. "There's more." Olive sat down in Anna's rocker and tried to take Karl on her lap. He stopped short, just before he reached the chair. Then he ran howling into the kitchen and out the back door. Startled, Susan turned to watch her sister's reaction, but Olive only looked after the little boy with a puzzled smile.

Susan took a quick breath and went back to the letter. "And I must tell you something that is a worry for me, too. Papa has wrenched his back. He insisted on helping with the piano. He took to his bed, but he will not let me call in Dr. Wendt. I must get the doctor to stop by for another reason."

"And to think we're so far away," Olive said, with a sigh. She leaned her head against the back of the chair. Her eyes were closed. Susan wished she could get her sister out of that chair.

"But Aunt Elviry is close, and Laura can help," Susan told her. "I'm just not going to let myself worry until I know there's something to worry about. That letter was written a week ago. Maybe he's better by now. Let's wait until we get another letter before we start to worry."

"Susan," Olive replied, "I wonder if you have any feelings for other people. First you leave Mama and Papa to marry Abe, and then you act this way when they have trouble." Olive's eyes were open now, and she frowned. The little worry lines were becoming permanently etched in her pale forehead.

Susan kept herself from reminding her sister of her own flight to Michigan's rich farmland when a promising suitor came along. "Olive," she said, smiling, "it's been a long time since you lived with Papa. Don't you remember how sick he gets when he feels blue? Maybe he did stretch a muscle, but I'll bet after that he got to thinking about me and the piano and how

I went away, and then he took to his bed.'' She paused, ''But Mama will bring him around! Just you see!''

''Well, you may be right, child,'' Olive said. ''Anyway, you'll have to use our wagon to bring the piano back from the station. That old wagon of Abe's will jolt it too much, especially with all the ruts in the road we seem to have every spring around here. Sometimes, Susan, I do miss the comforts I grew up with.''

Certainly Abe would not accept the proffered help. ''Oh, I think if we spread some rugs and some quilts on our wagon bed we'll get along just fine. I hope the weather holds. It would be just too bad if it rained!''

''It always rains in this part of the country in the spring, Susan. And then the tornadoes come. And after that the heat and mosquitoes.'' Olive rocked silently, gazing out of the window at the bleak fields beneath weak sunshine.

Susan looked at her sharply. The new worry lines made her sister look old and a little haggard. ''Are you feeling all right, Olive?'' she asked. ''Would it help if I took the children for a day or so? Maybe you need a rest.''

Olive sighed. ''No, no. The children are a comfort to me. I'm not really tired, I guess. But things do pile up, and living in this outlandish country makes it worse.'' She rocked, leaning her head back again and closing her eyes. ''I'd like to talk Joseph into moving to Milwaukee. Things would go better for us, both of us, in Milwaukee.'' She caressed the word, lingering over each syllable.

"But, Olive, Joseph would never do that. This section has some of the best farmland in the state, he always says." She watched Olive for a moment. "You'll feel better in a few weeks, and then everything else will seem easier, too."

Olive shook her head, her closed eyes not quite holding back tears she was trying to hide. "It's been coming on for a long time, Susan," she said. "Having you here cheered me up for a while, but there's no cure." She took a deep breath. "Joseph drinks, you know. And I cry. A fine household we have! I can't even hire help for myself. A hired girl would gossip about us."

Susan ran across the room and took her sister's hand. "But I'm here now, Olive. I'm here. Everything will work out." To herself she vowed, *I'll see that it does!*

She looked about her bright living room with its great roses trailing across the fresh wallpaper. Soon her curtain material would arrive. She would have a circle she could call her own. Anna would be outside it. Inside it, Susan would educate Abe to her own way of life and then reach out to help Olive and her babies, and even Joseph, too, if he would let her.

Only then would she begin to think of having children. Olive had started too soon, and now she was hemmed in, miserable, and even in danger of giving up.

"Olive," Susan said, "let's have a kind of party day after tomorrow! You and the boys can ride along into the village, and then we'll have a picnic after Abe and Joseph get the piano into the house. Maybe Fredrick could take some time off to help us, and he could eat the picnic with us, too. In those novels I read when I went away to school, people had picnics and parties all the time. Why shouldn't we?''

Olive patted her hand and sighed. ''Things never work out the way you think they will in this wild country. I sometimes wish Papa would help you out with some of that money he has made, since you and your husband are so poor. I just hope things turn out better here in Michigan for you than they have,'' she faltered, ''for Joseph and me.''

She rose heavily and started for the door. ''I'll see what Joseph says, though. Maybe I can bring the children over for the day. Maybe he won't mind. I doubt if he'll feel up to it, though.''

''Oh, Olive, don't *ask* him! Just say you're coming!''

Olive shook her head, but she smiled. ''Child, you have a lot to learn about living with a husband. Mama taught us housekeeping, but that's not enough. And Joseph's too old and set in his ways to change. Even last summer I still had some hopes, but now I don't know.''

Susan's optimism was boundless. ''Let me help you! Let *us* help you. Abe and I are strong. You'll see! Your children will grow up and make this land look just like the settled parts of the country, and then you and Joseph can go back to Prussia to visit—the way he's always said—and brag about your rich farm here.''

''Well, I must say, you do cheer a person up,'' Olive said, holding onto the doorpost to steady herself on the tipsy steps, "and I just may try to spend the day with you, whether Joseph can or not." Karl crept out from under the porch and ran to his mother.

As she watched her sister cross the yard and climb awkwardly over the rail fence, she recalled Abe's references to women's work, and to his desire for a large family soon. Then she remembered his quick, violent temper when she had crossed him.

But I won't let this kind of life beat me, she told herself. *And Abe's going to be my* partner *in fighting it. Mama had Indians for neighbors when she came to Milwaukee, and she didn't change, even though life for her was hardly the way it had been in the Old Country.*

She looked back through the open door to the living room. "Just wait until my piano comes," she said aloud. Her words were becoming a kind of litany. "Then this place will really be *my* house. *Mine!*"

She stared defiantly at Anna's rocking chair.

It remained still.

CHAPTER 12

TWO DAYS LATER AN April dawn promised pleasant, if chilly, air for their excursion. By seven, the cows were milked and put out to pasture, and the team of workhorses was brought up to the house so Susan could pile quilts and burlap bags onto the wagon bed. She and Abe ate a hasty breakfast of raised pancakes and bacon and applesauce, made from winter apples she had found buried in boxes of leaves.

Abe seemed as happy as Susan when he climbed up onto the wagon seat beside her and slapped the reins to start their horses toward the road.

"You deserve a little sunshine, Susan," he said, his eyes admiring her city bonnet and serge suit. She thought he just might pay her a compliment—for the first time—but he continued with, "You've been at it pretty hard these last days."

When they reached Joseph's house they found Olive and her children sitting in their buggy, ready to pull in behind them. Olive smiled and waved and little Karl took off his stocking cap and waved it at them, nearly falling over the side of the buggy.

"Let's have a parade!" cried Susan. "Let's stop for Fredrick Gerber, too, and he can come along back of the buggy on his horse. He can help you with the piano."

She was glad she was not near enough to hear Olive, probably murmuring, "What *will* the neighbors think!"

By the end of an hour, when they reached the outlying homes in the village and passed the blacksmith, who was already delivering a newly shod horse to a waiting customer, Susan could see train smoke in the distance. They pulled up at the station just as the train came to a chugging, puffing halt. A half-dozen merchants and farmers sat on the long porch that ran across the front of the unpainted frame building, or stood near the tracks chatting and exchanging local gossip. The train would bring a mail bag.

"You expecting a delivery this morning, Abe?" asked a man, whose name she had learned was Jake Gross. Jake helped to run the harness shop and acted as stationmaster whenever a train was due to stop.

"Good morning, Mrs. Braun," he called to Olive. Then to Fredrick he made a ribald remark in Low Dutch. Susan didn't understand, but she saw Olive's back stiffen and felt embarrassed for her, as Abe chuckled along with the rest.

Then he introduced Susan to Jake and to the other neighbors near by. For a few minutes, before they all turned to their deliveries from the train, Susan became

93

the center of attention. Curious eyes evaluated Abe's choice of a bride, but his joking, comfortable way with the men eased her introduction to his world. She was glad she had worn her bonnet with blue velvet trim. She knew it set off her blue eyes and fair hair.

"It's Susan's piano we're here for," he explained to Jake, "and a trunk, too, I believe. We'd be much obliged if you'd help us get them onto the wagon."

"A piano! You'll be asked to have a Sunday-night sing at your house between the pastor's rounds if you don't watch out, Susan!" Jake grinned at her in an open, friendly way. He wore his brown felt hat far back on his head and his thick blond hair swept into his snapping blue eyes.

Susan could not respond to such familiarity. In all her life she had not heard any neighbor call her mother by her first name. She smiled faintly and then she looked at Abe. He did not seem aware of her discomfort. She knew she must not fail him now, though, and have his friends think she was flaunting her High German background.

She turned quickly to Jake while Abe began checking the interior of the first baggage car. "Abe didn't tell me about that." She smiled again, but she was not able to call this stranger by his first name. "It will be a pleasure for us to have the congregation at our home on a Sunday evening soon," she said.

"Well, Jake, as long as you're going to be listening to that piano, you can help us start it on its way!" Abe said, chuckling. He jumped out of the third car, where he had found Susan's belongings.

Soon there were several men easing the box with

her square piano out of the car and onto the wagon bed. Her piano was old-fashioned, she knew, but she loved it, and she caressed it with her eyes. Newer pianos might be smaller and more graceful, but this one was *hers*.

Fredrick brought out her big trunk. At seventeen, he was all awkward elbows and big feet. But he managed his load without dropping it.

"Maybe a stein at Herman's would taste good, Abe." Susan turned to see a young man with a full, blond beard, grinning at them.

"Maybe it would," growled Abe. "Why don't you go over there and find out? I got this load to get home, and at a slow walk, too." He looked toward Susan and then toward the village. "Anyway, much obliged," he added, in Low German.

"Who's Herman?" Susan whispered to Olive, who had come to sit with her while Karl ran about among the men, now unloading their own mail and packages.

"Herman runs the saloon," Olive replied, and she added bitterly, "I don't know him very well, but of course Joseph knows him—too well."

Susan wanted to ask if Abe went there, too, but she could not bring the words out. She really did not want to hear, not on a day that promised to be so fair in so many ways.

After her trunk and piano were securely tied, she climbed into the buggy with Olive, who held the baby on her lap. Karl jumped up on the wagon seat with Abe, and Fredrick took the lead, his shaggy black head bare atop his scarecrow frame. He rode with a blanket thrown over the back of a plow horse.

Susan winced when Abe slapped the reins and the wagon jolted through a mud puddle along the tracks, shaking its load. Then she clucked quietly to her horse, and he followed the wagon's lead. Karl bounced and chattered and waved back at them.

"How Laura would love this!" cried Susan. "I must invite her to visit us this summer. And Mama, too." She began making plans again, humming to herself.

"Olive, will you come over on Sunday nights if the other neighbors do?"

"We'll see," her sister murmured. "You know," she went on, "it won't be like gatherings in Mama's parlor. You'll have to install a spittoon, for one thing, for all that flying tobacco juice."

Susan looked at her, horrified. "You're making jokes. *You* had neighbors in last summer and you didn't have a spittoon.

"But I chose the ones I asked. If you have a Sunday-night sing, anybody in the congregation can come. And they will. And they'll tell jokes that you won't want to hear—in Low Dutch—and they'll sing Bavarian gospel songs until your head will swim! And then they'll start on saloon songs."

"Even with their wives and children along?"

"I don't think these peasants know what good manners are."

"But Abe's not like that." While defending him before Olive she forgot the last few weeks' misgivings about his annoying habits. She was sure she could educate him to her ways.

Olive was silent, and her silence infuriated Susan.

"He's not! He's had some schooling. And Mr. Spencer, who raised him, taught him to speak good English. He doesn't even have as much accent as Adolph—or as Papa, for that matter." She wanted to add "or as Joseph," but she did not dare.

Olive sighed, and then she shifted her body awkwardly on the buggy seat. "Of course, child, of course, But blood will tell, you know."

Susan forgot her determination to be happy all the day. She stormed, "What kind of 'blood' did President Lincoln have, pray tell, sister? You forget yourself!" She stopped, glancing at Olive's dour face, suddenly realizing her sister's mounting problems probably gave her a negative outlook on life in general.

"Oh, Olive," she cried, "let's not fight! We have to stick together, you and I!"

Olive looked at her with surprise. "I guess that's right. I do have *you* now."

Then she took a deep breath of the spring air, already faintly fragrant with turned soil, and glanced about the countryside. It was finally beginning to show small patches of green in fence corners and on willow trees. She pushed the baby's stocking cap back so he could get some of the fresh air, warming now in the midday sunshine.

"It will be a *fine* day for a picnic, Susan." She smiled, and her frown lines smoothed out. "I'm glad I decided to come."

I know what I'll do, Susan thought, staring at Abe's back as though she could communicate with him. *I'll tell Abe to get those men to leave their chewing to-*

bacco at home, and that way I'll teach him some manners, too.

In her heart she knew Abe would never tell his friends how to behave, but now she deliberately filed her misgivings away.

When they arrived at Olive's house, Joseph was coming off the porch and he turned toward the barn. But then he stopped to stare at their parade, his watery blue eyes and ginger beard, the only spots of color in his pale face.

"Joseph!" cried Susan. "Climb on the back of the wagon. Have your dinner with us! I want you to sing some songs with me at my piano." She halted her horse.

Joseph grunted. He seemed sober. "You're wasting a good workday, Abe," he grumbled, coming toward the road. He shook his head, but he put his foot on a spoke of the wagon wheel and hoisted himself up. "I'd have to eat cold potatoes by myself, so I guess I might just as well come along," he said, with a sigh.

As they started off again, Olive whispered, "How do you suppose he timed his trip out to the barn just right so he could see us go by? He can't fool me!" But she was obviously glad to have him along.

Toward noon spring rain clouds threatened their picnic, so Susan laid out on the kitchen table their ham and potatoes baked in milk Susan had left in the warm oven after breakfast. The rich, sweet aroma had met them when they opened the door. Karl ran down to the cellar for cucumber pickles. Olive brought in their dessert—a fresh sour cream *kuchen* she had wrapped in a kitchen towel.

They could hear the men beginning to unload the wagon, and just before she went into the living room to supervise the entry of her piano, Susan placed a flaming red geranium plant in the center of the green oilcloth.

"As soon as I can get into the trunk for my linens," she told Olive, "I'll have a pretty table, even it it's only a kitchen table."

"And more work for yourself, too, washing table-cloths," replied Olive.

Susan passed up a chance to argue over that remark as she opened the door to the living room and saw her piano already in the spot she had saved for it.

Her buoyancy sustained her through their dinner. Abe responded to her laughter and so did Fredrick and little Karl.

"Mama," he begged, munching on his large piece of kuchen, "can't I stay here with Aunt Susan? I'm too big to take a nap any more. I can even walk home by myself." His round blue eyes peered up through shaggy bangs.

"Indeed you may not," replied his mother. "It's not good manners to invite oneself."

"Oh, Olive," said Susan, "let him stay. I'd love to have him. The house is lonely here for me."

"Well," Olive faltered, "he really should have a nap, but—"

Joseph spoke up for the first time. "You are to come home with us, Karl. Let us hear no more about it."

No one said anything. Tears started to make their way down the little boy's fat cheeks.

Then Fredrick laughed, pushing Karl's silky bangs out of his eyes. "Hey, old man," he said, "You was gonna help me hitch up that team. Right? You can't leave me do it all by myself!"

Karl swallowed a sob and began on his breadcake again, digging his tongue into the dollops of thick cream on the top. His adoring eyes transferred from Susan to Fredrick.

He needs to have somebody hug him, Susan told herself. *I must see to that.*

She rose and began clearing the table.

After Abe and Joseph and Fredrick had gone into the fields to begin planting wheat, and Olive had gone home to put the children to bed for their naps, Susan washed the dishes and then she sat down at her piano again. There had been little time for songs. The polished wood and ivory keys gleamed. The rich color of Adolph's red wool lap robe complemented her newly bright walls.

Now the living room was hers, and the kitchen was hers. With the cotton material her mother had sent, there would soon be new curtains.

But the bedroom, the bedroom where Anna had slept—and died—while Abe listened to her coughing from his cot in the loft, was still not hers. Her own linens, not the cheap ones they had bought in the village soon after they moved in, would help.

Only when she had drawn her circle around the bedroom, too, and made it a part of her personal domain, would she feel secure.

That's part of Olive's trouble, thought Susan.

Joseph runs everything over there, and sometimes he's just not capable of making decisions. Women have to carry children and take care of them, too, and they should decide when to have them.

Out of the corner of her eye she saw a slight movement of the rocker. Then the floorboard beneath it creaked.

"In spite of the piano," the chair seemed to say, "*this* room is still mine, too."

Susan rose at once. Turning her back on the chair, she ran outdoors to begin her afternoon chores—bringing in wood and water, feeding the chickens and gathering eggs, and straining the curds from the whey she had waiting in the cellar. She would make Dutch cheese from the curds for supper.

When she went by the living room door she glanced in. This time her piano and Anna's rocking chair looked quiet and serene together.

She talked to herself while she worked, taking up her old problem again. "But when Abe is too tired or too busy to be interested in me for a few days—oh, I wish I could talk to Olive about such things—but look at what a mess she's made of her life—or to Mama. Imagine! Mama didn't tell me anything.

"Somewhere women must know about ways a woman can live with a man and not bring a lot of children into the world. I guess I'll just have to talk to Abe again. He'll be embarrassed, and so will I. But that's another job I'll need to take on. And soon. Talking to him about the rocker and about those awful noises will have to wait."

Susan sank into a kitchen chair by the table, a chair

that faced away from the living room door. She sighed.

I know Anna's gone—in her grave in that little orchard—and she can't hurt me or any of us. And why would she want to? I'm not trying to destoy Abe's memories of her. I just want to give him some others—some happier ones. But it did give me a turn, she thought, *to see Olive rocking today in there, and looking sick, too.*

CHAPTER 13

AFTER SUSAN'S PIANO became a resident of the living room, the chair rocked every day. It never seemed to stir in the morning while Abe was still in the house, or at noon during their dinner. Even in the evening, when the days began to lengthen, and during their supper when one could begin to make out shadowy forms in the living room—beyond the reach of the oil lamp —there was never any movement or any sound of creaking floorboards.

At night, when Abe finally came in from his chores, he and Susan usually read, or Susan darned socks by the kitchen table. And all was quiet then, too, inside the house and out, except for an occasional bawling cow or whinnying horse or the soft hooting of a barn owl.

But every day, in the late afternoon, before Abe returned, a slight rhythmic movement signaled the creaking boards beneath Anna's little chair. One morning Susan dragged the rocker to the other side of the room. Then she stood, and swayed, and finally stamped on the floor where the chair usually sat. The boards were firm. She moved the chair back. But that afternoon, while she sewed at the kitchen table, the familiar creaking sound floated out as usual from the living room.

For the next few days Susan looked for work outside the house during the late afternoon hours. She cleaned lamps and polished their chimneys on the back porch, or she gathered eggs and tended setting hens, or she carried sticks of wood Abe had split to the wood box. Sometimes, though, she played her piano. The soft glow of its keyboard and its gleaming wood and true, sonorous notes from its fine sounding board brightened the room, even when rain brought early darkness. The chair was quiet while Susan played her piano.

And if she approached it, to still its rocking, the chair stopped moving. When she dusted it or pushed it aside to clean the faded rag rug that covered that part of the floor, its smooth pine in her hands felt like any other wood.

I've never been the kind of person who imagines things, she told herself. *This is just not like me.* She tried to smile a little when she recalled the way she had scoffed at her brother's letter, warning about Bavarian ghosts and advising her not to marry Abe. *I do wish I could talk to somebody about the chair, though,* she thought, *and we could laugh about that silly rocking. I'll bet laughing at it would help a whole lot.*

But Susan feared Olive and her mother would worry

about her sanity—and she could imagine Abe's reaction!

One rainy morning Abe sat on a stool on the dirt floor in the cellar and cut the eyes from potatoes. Susan, who was churning butter in the kitchen, could hear him singing while he worked. In order to hear better, she opened the cellar door, which led to a small lean-to at the back of the house where steps went down to the cellar. Abe was singing German drinking songs, the kind Olive told Susan neighbors might bellow out at the end of a hymn-sing in someone's home. The strong rhythms and coarse words at first repelled her.

But then her body began to respond to their lilt. By the time Abe brought the potato parts he could not use—already scrubbed and ready for cooking—to the kitchen, whole phrases and bits of melody were charging through her brain. Susan longed for a chance to get to her piano to play those dancing notes.

"Abe," she said, laughing, "come right into the living room with me. I'll play those songs for you. Now! Before I lose them!"

Abe smiled. "Was I pretty loud? I guess I felt good today. Having you here with me is good for me, Susan. I guess I was making a few plans for us, too."

He followed her toward the living room. "It's a lot better, let me tell you, a lot better than," he paused at the door, and then he continued slowly, "better than last year just at this time." Then he stopped abruptly and leaned against the doorpost.

Susan was already on the piano stool. She had leaned over to begin to pick out an elusive melody before she heard Abe say, "Susan, maybe we could

wait until another day to sing those songs together."
He turned back to the kitchen.

She ignored him while she tried a line or two,
humming along to help her recall the tune. It was the
first fun she'd had at the piano in a long time.

Abe broke into her concentration. "Susan!" he
thundered.

Startled, she looked up to see him sitting at the
kitchen table with his back to her. He was leaning his
head on his hand.

The old guilt she knew from childhood, built from
fearing she had done *something* wrong, somehow,
whenever an adult shouted, made her spring up from
the piano stool at once. "Whatever is the matter,
Abe?" she asked.

Neither of them moved for a moment. Then Abe
said, in a broken voice, "I didn't mean to talk like
that, Susan. It just came out that way." He turned his
head toward the living room, but he did not look into
it, or at her. "I believe the rain is over, Susan," he
went on. "I can plant those potatoes this afternoon, I
guess. If you would fix us some dinner now, I could
start as soon as we are through eating."

Puzzled, but glad to see his anger gone, Susan
checked the potato parts Abe had put into a large pot
on the stove. As she went down to the cellar for a
crock of sausage from a pig Abe had killed in February, all at once she realized what she had done—
what they had done.

She and Abe were going to sing ribald songs together in Anna's living room on what must be a year
after the very day she had died.

Abe was silent during dinner. Susan, by turns sorry for him and then annoyed at his refusal to talk to her about his grief, managed to keep quiet. At last, though, she felt she had to know.

"Was it today—a year ago—Abe?" she asked him.

Abe did not look at her. He stared into the coffee cup in his hand. "A year ago today I thought my life was over," he said at last. Then he looked up. "Can you imagine how I felt a little while ago when I realized I'd forgotten the date? Already? She wouldn't have forgotten me this soon, Susan."

Abe rose heavily and put on his old wool jacket and hat. Susan watched him as he picked up the crate of potatoes on the porch and walked slowly toward the field west of the house.

But you forgot for a while, Abe, she said to herself, after he had gone. *I helped you forget for a while. And by the time another anniversary of Anna's death comes around, maybe I'll have made your life so much better I'll even have to remind you.*

Just when Susan was putting the last of the clean dishes into the cupboard, she heard a knock on the back door. It was the first time a stranger had stopped at the house, and stories of gypsy bands and of battle-distraught tramps still wandering the countryside long after the Great Civil War flashed through her mind. She peeked apprehensively through her new yellow curtains.

The little man on the porch had a long red beard, and his black felt hat brim rode low over his wiry eyebrows. One eye was missing, and its sunken lids were slightly parted. On the whole, however, he looked rather young and quite harmless.

"How-de-do, ma'am," he said when she opened the door. He took his hat off to reveal a great shock of red hair. His accent was Yankee, not German.

"I have on the road yonder, as you may see, ma'am, a cart with dry goods, threads, and some small furniture pieces. And I would inquire of you, do you have a need for the purchase of any of these products? Or possibly, you might be of a mind to sell me an article of your own, for which you no longer have a use."

Susan knew she must not ask him in. But it seemed good to hear a stranger talk. She had not realized how much she missed that aspect of her parents' busy household and of her school days in Milwaukee.

"I have a coffeepot on the stove," she said. "Just sit down there on the step and I'll bring a cup out to the porch."

She stood next to him while he sat and drank from the tin cup. He began to talk about the weather and the planting. He must lead a lonely life, too, she thought.

"I'm afraid there's nothing I need," Susan told him. "My mother just recently sent me a well-packed trunk from Milwaukee. And I do have very little spending money as it is."

"Your neighbor on the next road walks into the city, fifteen miles each way, with a basket of eggs to sell, every Saturday, ma'am, through drifts and storms alike. She is a wealthy woman, let me tell you. She bought silk threads and a new thimble from me this morning. When you have lived here longer, you will have your own income, too, from your hens and from your garden.''

Susan had heard about the enterprising woman who lived on a farm next to Olive and Joseph. Her six well-trained children took care of the house and helped her husband while she sewed and raised chickens.

''Maybe,'' she told the young man, ''someday I'll have spending money, too, then. But not today, I'm afraid.''

''Things do seem brighter around here than they did the last two years I've come through, ma'am,'' he said. ''The poor, sick creature who came to your door in those days looked as though she could have used a little silk thread to cheer her up. Perhaps you are caring for her?''

''That was my husband's sister,'' Susan answered. She paused. ''She—she's dead now.''

The man rose with a sigh and handed her the tin cup. ''Well, that's the way it goes. In every household I visit, out in this wild countryside, it is the same. There are always one or two missing from the year before. Much obliged for the coffee, ma'am.''

Susan crossed the kitchen to watch him climb onto his little cart and slap the reins on the back of his old horse. Atop the load of merchandise sat a small wooden rocking chair.

All at once Susan knew what to do with Anna's chair. She ran to the door to call him back.

But then a vision of Abe's stricken face during their dinner an hour earlier stopped her. It was too soon.

But by next year, she told herself, *if that chair*

109

hasn't calmed down, somehow I will have prepared Abe to let me get rid of it.

She sighed. *At least it doesn't do anyone any harm, though. Just rocking a little now and then in there,* she thought.

Susan glanced into the living room. A faint ray of sunshine broke through the clouds, sending its beam across the quiet rocking chair.

CHAPTER 14

HOWEVER, DURING THE NEXT few days Susan had little time to spend with Abe. He worked long, exhausting hours in the fields and she planted her garden and sewed and waited for his return for their evening meal, long after dark.

The gently rocking chair was a constant presence, but the moans of her first night in the house never disturbed her again, and she seldom listened for them now.

Joseph took an interest in the planting and cultivating, so he was happier.

Susan wrote her mother a glowing letter about her sister and her sister's husband and their family.

"Life in Michigan is hard, Mama," she conceded, "but we are all content here, and Olive's children are thriving."

She was not really lying, Susan decided, but only shading the truth a bit. That would give her mother some comfort. And comfort her own mind a little, too.

Olive, however, was growing more and more depressed. She dragged herself about to take care of the children. There were dark circles beneath her eyes, and the news from Milwaukee that their father had not risen from his sickbed was constantly on her mind.

One sultry afternoon in early June, Susan put on her sunbonnet and walked over to see her sister with some pale, tender lettuce she had cut. She found Olive lying on the big walnut bed in her bedroom.

"I thought I'd rest while the boys took their naps," apologized her sister. "This hot weather is too much for me. I hope it rains before night."

She wiped her perspiring forehead with a corner of her apron and brushed back Karl's damp hair. He was dozing next to her, his fat legs sprawling on the quilt.

Susan dropped into the little rocker next to the window. "There are thunderheads in the west, Olive," she said. "All the men will have to be in early today. Maybe I can get your supper before I leave. Abe will have to wait for a few minutes for once, I guess."

Even as Susan spoke, thunder shook the drooping, hot branches outside the window and a great streak flashed across the darkening sky. The heavy still air seemed about to smother them all.

She watched Joseph and Fredrick hurriedly bringing a half load of hay into the barn as a spatter of rain began. The livid sky fascinated her and she saw the men looking up, too, toward giant black clouds in the west.

Then Fredrick, who was closing the sliding door to

the haymow, pointed at something, and they both started running toward the house. Susan saw it at almost the same time. An ugly, snake-like swirl of dust, narrow at the bottom but twisting toward a great funnel shape at the top, tore across the fields in a mass of violent monstrous energy.

Susan turned breathlessly toward Olive, who was leaning over the cradle, trying to soothe her whimpering baby. Susan snatched little Karl, rousing him, hot and irritated, from his nap, and cried, "It's a tornado! Carry the baby to the fruit cellar! I'll take Karl!"

She dashed out the kitchen door, holding the struggling child close to her, and around the house to the horizontal fruit cellar door. Fredrick was there before her. She could never have forced the heavy door open in the great gusts of wind by herself, but he held it for her while she and Karl ran down into the darkness.

Then Joseph was standing on the top step, peering at them through the gloom. Above the rising wind he shouted, "Where are the others?"

"Right behind me!" cried Susan.

The atmosphere outside was nearly as black as that in the cellar. She could make out Fredrick's figure, standing on a step, still holding the door with both hands braced against it. Then a mighty gust blew it shut, hurling both men to the bottom of the stairs next to the spot where Susan and Karl crouched, their arms about each other.

Before Joseph could pick himself up and try to reach the opening again, there was a flash of light that

113

penetrated the cracks in the wooden door, accompanied by a crash that rocked the house overhead. And then finally it was quiet, except for wind-swept rain pelting the outside of the door and a distant roll of thunder.

An acrid odor filled the cellar.

"Olive! Olive!" called Joseph, stumbling up the wooden stairs. Susan followed the men. Karl held her hand tightly, calling, "Mama!"

There was no more wind. Fredrick pushed the overhead door open easily.

Then Susan saw her sister, stretched out on the ground under a branch of the elm tree that had hung over the door to the fruit cellar. The elm was split down the middle. Olive must have been trying to reach the horizontal door when a lightning bolt hit as she passed underneath, or as she stood trying to lift the door against the wind.

The baby, thrown free, was wailing. Olive lay still.

While Joseph and Fredrick bent over Olive, Susan took up the sobbing baby and tried to comfort him. "There, there," she whispered, through her tears.

Only then did she think to look toward her own home, toward Abe, east of Joseph's farm, and directly in the path of the tornado.

Holding the baby and leaping over fallen branches along the way, Susan ran like a wild woman across the soggy yard and climbed the fence next to the barn. She stood on the top rail, shading her eyes with her hand, and peered through the dim light.

The house was still there, and so was the barn. She could follow the erratic path of the tornado as it twisted across woods and fields. It had moved north just before it would have reached her home. Surely Abe was safe, too, for their fields lay to the south of the tornado's path.

Susan sat on the top rail and wept. She held Olive's baby tightly to herself while she rocked back and forth and cried, until she felt she could go back to Joseph and somehow try to comfort him.

She found Joseph nearly beside himself with grief. Fredrick was riding bareback down the muddy road, pounding his heels into the sides of a now-galloping workhorse he had unhitched a few minutes before. He looked like a crouching scarecrow atop the terrified horse.

"Fredrick's going to get Doc Hosmer. Here, Susan," cried Joseph, "help me take her inside to her bed. Maybe she'll come around." He peered into her white, drawn face. "Some do, you know."

Susan ran to put the baby into his cradle and then sped back to find Joseph, his arms around his wife's waist, dragging her toward the door. Karl followed, sucking his thumb and sobbing. Joseph was small and ailing, and Olive, her head drooping grotesquely from her heavy, limp body, was too much for him to pick up and carry. Susan lifted Olive's soggy legs and they made their way into the house.

They laid Olive on the big bed, her wet clothing and streaming hair instantly soaking the quilt. The child that would soon have come into the world lay quiet, too, inside a little mound under her clammy print apron. The baby sobbed in his cradle and Karl—round-eyed and clinging to the slats of the cradle—stared at his mother's still body.

"Susan, I can't put up with this." Joseph stumbled toward the door to the kitchen. "What is there left for me? Only to curse God and die!"

Susan, who was holding her sister's hand and smoothing back her dark gold hair from her face, realized what he meant to do.

"Oh, Joseph, don't take even one little sip!" she said. "What will we do? What will the little ones do? Look at poor Karl!"

Joseph stopped at the door and stared at his children. With a mighty effort he turned back. He picked the little boy up, holding him close. The gesture seemed to give him courage. "Maybe Doc can do something after all," he said finally. "And I guess it wouldn't be right not to be in good shape when he gets here."

Susan sighed. One more bridge crossed. She prayed for help in the crises she knew would come in the next days and weeks.

She looked about her at the little family, everyone with eyes fastened on the body of the woman who had held their lives together. The baby drew himself up to peer at Olive through the crib rails. "Mu-muh?" he gurgled, his chubby face breaking into a grin. He had not tried to talk before, though Olive and Susan teased and encouraged him day after day.

Karl began to laugh. "He did it, Aunt Susan! Tell Mama she should listen. Tell her!"

Susan could bear no more. She swept past Joseph, who was still standing in the bedroom doorway, and out to the wet, branch-strewn porch. Two of the rails lay shattered on the lawn.

116

I've got to get away, she told herself, *if only for a little while.* She ran down the steps and started toward the road, her damp skirts cold against her wet stockings.

But then she stopped. Her body became taut. She stood for a moment with her eyes closed and her fists clenched. *I'm no better than poor Joseph,* she told herself, *trying to run away like this.* Her old formula returned. *What would Mama do? And what would Mama say if she could see me deserting Olive's children now?*

With a sigh she turned herself around and squared her shoulders. Then with a swift movement she tidied her damp, windblown hair and fastened it securely again into its tight bun.

Just as she was starting up the porch steps she heard Abe's welcome voice from the road. "Susan? Susan! Oh, Susan, thank the Lord!" he continued as he ran to her, out of breath and smiling in his slow, all-encompassing way that lighted up his eyes and seemed to come from deep within him.

But then he looked at her closely and his smile died. "Things are not good here?" he asked.

Susan felt part of her burden that had seemed too heavy to bear shift a little. Abe was here. She was not alone.

Numb from her emotional turmoil, Susan could only shake her head and motion her husband into the house. He followed her with questions in his eyes but he said nothing more until he saw Olive.

"This is too bad. Just too bad," Abe murmured quietly to Joseph, who still stood in the doorway, his

117

eyes glazed and tears streaming down his cheeks into his sparse beard. The momentary happiness of the little boys had sunk into silence.

"Uncle Abe," cried Karl, "Mama's sick. Can't I go home with you? I'll be good. Can't I, Aunt Susan?"

Joseph roused himself. "No, Karl. No. You will stay here." He turned, sobbing, toward Susan. "You will not take them, Susan. The boys are all I've got."

"Just for tonight, Joseph. The doctor will come and then after that surely neighbors will drop by."

"No." His small chin jutted forward. "No, Susan. We need to be together now." Joseph picked up the baby, and then Karl, who looked at his father in wonder. Joseph had seldom touched the children. "You go home, too, Susan. We'll manage." His voice rose. "That's the way it will be. Let us hear no more."

Susan started to tell him he could not possibly manage alone, but Abe interrupted her.

"Joseph," he said, "we'll leave you now. Try to think what Olive would want. She would want the boys looked after. Just rest a little and try to think. Susan and I will be out there in the kitchen when you need us."

Susan left the room with a picture in her mind she knew would always shape her thinking about her new life.

The bright June sun and lush smells of fresh-cut hay and of field roses growing on a wire frame outside the window made a lie of the devastation of the past hour. Still-dripping branches and parts of the barn roof lay scattered through the yard.

Susan stood by the kitchen window next to the porch, her arms folded. Fredrick should be back soon with the doctor. Abe strode over to the table, pulled a chair out, and sank into it. He put one elbow on the table and shaded his eyes with his hand.

Susan began to find words. "Abe, Mama was right. So was Karl and so was Reverend Schneider. They were all right. This is wild country."

Abe sighed but he said nothing.

"I've told you before, you know. It killed your Mama and Papa and it killed your sister Anna. And now it's killed Olive, too." She began to realize the enormity of their loss. "And look at what it's done to Joseph. He wouldn't be drinking all the time to get away from his problems and maybe destroy his poor motherless children, too, if he lived in Prussia. Or even in Milwaukee. People don't do that in civilized places."

Abe roused himself briefly, his dark eyes seeking hers. "They do, Susan," he said. "People do those things in other places."

She continued to stare out the window. "No, they don't! Not in *our* family. Mama always said we don't have drunkards in *our* family." She turned to him. "And look what happened to Olive even before she—" Susan could not yet use the word—"while she was still alive. She was so *sad* all the time. Olive was never like that before. Olive was always happy and singing and making plans. Just like me. Just the way *I* do. And then she got to be like—like the way you say Anna was."

Abe rose quickly and walked to the sunny window

119

across the room. He thrust his fists deep into his pockets.

Susan went recklessly on. "Anna was sick and you told me you had to decide things for her. Well, Joseph couldn't decide for Olive. This wild country beat them both, Abe. And it beat Anna, too, because—"

Abe's voice was harsh. "That will do, Susan." He cleared his throat and sighed again, deeply. "Now that you talked it out, maybe you'll feel better. Just be quiet now, Susan."

Susan closed her mouth tightly. Somehow, hurting Abe after Olive's death had helped her soothe her own growing despair.

She leaned her head against the window frame. *Now that I've gone and acted like a child again,* she told herself, *I'll have to take on a woman's work here for a while.*

CHAPTER 15

FREDRICK BROUGHT HIS MOTHER back with him. Susan was sitting in a wooden rocking chair on the porch, waiting for Dr. Hosmer, when she saw Mrs. Gerber—on Joseph's plowhorse Fritz—turn into the driveway. Fredrick walked alongside.

Mrs. Gerber got off the horse with some difficulty. She was short and stout, with round red cheeks and a firm, healthy body that, Susan knew, often shook with spontaneous laughter. Fredrick had to reach up to help her slide her feet down onto the block near the porch.

"I figured you could use some neighboring here, Mrs. Hesse," Fredrick said, "so I stopped on the way back and picked up Ma. When I got to Doc Hosmer's, he'd just pulled into his yard. There was twins born down in the swamp this afternoon. Stillborn, they was, he said. He felt real bad when he heard about Mrs. Braun. Said it probably won't do no good, but he'll be along anyhow."

"It was kind of you to come, Mrs. Gerber," Susan said, rising to greet Fredrick's mother. "Abe had to go home to take care of the chores. And Joseph—" Susan swallowed quickly before going on to discuss a family problem with a relative stranger. "Joseph just sits there by the bed, holding the boys. When I try to take them away—the baby needs changing—Joseph only says, 'In a minute, Susan. Let us be together a little longer.' I can hardly stand to see it, Mrs. Gerber."

Susan sat down again. With an effort she kept her voice even and controlled. But when she described the scene in the bedroom, their loss overwhelmed her once more.

"There, there, child," Mrs. Gerber said. She did not touch Susan, not even to take her hand. But the woman's strength and vitality seemed to radiate and encompass the whole stricken household. "Just rest yourself here for a little. It's a bad time, that's sure. But let me see what I can do."

She went into the house and Fredrick took the path to the barn.

Susan sat briefly, but soon she rose again and started to pace back and forth along the white wooden porch.

A few moments later she heard quiet conversation, and then footsteps. She knew she should go inside to help Mrs. Gerber, but she could not will herself to look at those faces in the bedroom again.

She stopped pacing and gazed out into the yard.

Great slashes showed where lightning had split the giant elm by the fruit cellar door. Two elms between the house and the barn were uprooted, and there were branches and twigs and shingles from the barn everywhere. She looked for the small smokehouse that had stood beyond an old oak. There was no trace of it. Debris, largely ears of corn and slats from the corncrib that seemed to have been dumped on that one spot, covered its foundations. All evidence of the drenching rain that had accompanied the tornado was gone, too, in the afternoon heat, except for a few puddles in the road.

At last Mrs. Gerber appeared in the doorway, with the drowsy baby on her hip. Karl's hand was in hers. His tear-streaked face showed only bewilderment.

"Now then, you sit here with your Aunt Susan, Karly," she said, "while I put your little brother down for his nap in your Mama's guest room. Mr. Braun is taking a rest on the sofa, Mrs. Hesse. I think it might be a good idea if you just stay on the porch and watch for Doc Hosmer. Fredrick's at the barn already, so you don't need to worry yourself about the chores, either."

Susan made herself focus on small problems. Hugging Karl. Trying to assess the damage outside the house.

"Mrs. Gerber," she said, turning again to the porch rail, "look at the devastation. I've never seen anything like it. And it's as though the tornado just concentrated on this one home, isn't it?"

Mrs. Gerber came over to stand beside her. Susan reached down for Karl's other hand. He gave her his hot, damp hand, but he did not cling to her.

"*Ja*, well," the woman said, "that's the way these

123

twisters act. Our place wasn't hit this time, though, thank the Lord. And yours? Is everything all right with you folks?''

"Yes," Susan said, reluctant to let her mind even consider alternatives. "The tornado went off to the north after it hit here, I guess."

"Well, now, that means the old Spencer place was in its way. I hope they didn't have any bad luck over there."

". . . wasn't hit *this* time." ". . . bad luck over there." Susan could stand no more.

"Oh, Mrs. Gerber," she said, "is living here always so harsh and so—insecure?''

Karl took his hand from hers and put his thumb into his mouth. He kept hold of the older woman, though, and moved closer to her.

"*Ach,* you're nothing more than a child yourself, at that," Mrs. Gerber said, looking closely at Susan. She shifted the baby, holding the sleeping boy now with his tousled head against her shoulder. "Of course," she went on, "it's no different here than any place else in the world. Back in the Old Country we had to worry about our men getting conscripted. And in the Old Country there were other men who never did a day's work in their lives. Nor did their fathers. Nor their grandfathers before them. But *those* men ran *our* lives. And besides having to put up with *them,* we had to put up with ordinary rampages of nature, too.''

She sighed, a contented sigh. "I suppose it's hard for you to see it on a bad day like this one, Mrs. Hesse, but what we've got here in this country is good. Folks like us couldn't do no better.''

124

But I could, Susan thought. *And my children could. And my husband. Mrs. Gerber looks at things from a peasant's point of view.* She caught herself. Abe was a "peasant," too, then.

Her old determination to direct her life—and the lives of those around her—began to return. She squared her shoulders.

"Mrs. Gerber, you're right," she said, picking Karl up and brushing back his bangs. "If you can get the baby settled down, I'll start supper. Dr. Hosmer may want a bite to eat before he goes back to town. And then this evening I suppose neighbors will stop by." She paused. "I believe I'll stir up a spice cake.

"After that," she swallowed a lump in her throat, "if you would help me take care of Olive, I'd be awfully grateful."

Mrs. Gerber smiled. "I always knew you two sisters had gumption. That young woman lying in there was a real credit to your ma, Mrs. Hesse. And you are, too. You tell your ma I said that when you write her, do you hear? Tell her that."

Susan passed the next few hours in a kind of trance.

After the doctor's call Abe sent Fredrick back to the village with a message to go by telegraph to South Milwaukee. Along the way Fredrick stopped to tell neighbors the sad news as Abe had instructed him. He paid a visit to the tavern, too, and spread the word among the men who came in for an early evening stein of beer. They all knew Joseph. They and their wives would attend the funeral Joseph had decided would take place in his parlor two days after Olive's death.

Finally Fredrick stopped to see the pastor. Reverend

Schwenk followed Fredrick back to the Brauns' at once in his buggy.

When Susan watched Joseph greet visitors and make one difficult decision after another, she saw for the first time a gracious, capable man she knew Olive had remembered and loved. He went through his wife's clothing and laid out Olive's new lavender dimity shirtwaist.

Then Susan and Mrs. Gerber washed the body and dressed it. The two women cried together over the pretty woman and the obvious evidence of a second lost life—evidence they did not try to camouflage with a shawl. And then Abe and Joseph carried Olive's body to the mohair couch in the parlor.

"Tomorrow," Abe said, "I will make the coffin. Let me do that for her."

Susan realized, with a flash of pleasure, Joseph was talking to Abe as an equal. "Abe," he asked, "can you spare the time to sit up with me tonight? By tomorrow night others will know and some of them may offer to help out."

"I'd planned on doing that anyway, Joseph," Abe said. "If it hadn't been here in your parlor I'd be sitting, it would have been at home in my kitchen I'd keep watch. And Joseph," he added, "let me bring over some of my cider."

Joseph sighed. "I think we'll drink coffee tonight, Abe, if that's all right with you." He paused. "Olive would have wanted us to drink coffee, I think."

By ten o'clock the pastor and most of the neighbors had left. Albert Rouse, a deacon in the Lutheran

126

Church and a friend of Joseph's—a big man with a curly gray beard—and his son George—a quiet, dark young fellow with a farm just outside the village—had offered to sit by the body with Joseph and Abe. Susan kept to herself in the kitchen after Mrs. Gerber left. She let Karl stay up with her until he fell asleep over a picture book at the kitchen table. With Olive's body out of the bedroom, she put the baby back into his cradle. At Joseph's insistence, she made the bed up with fresh sheets and tucked Karl into the covers in his parents' bed.

"He will always be near me now," Joseph said. "And the baby, too. We must stay together."

Susan found a prayer book Olive had kept in the top drawer of a dresser in the dining room. She wrapped her sister's crocheted shawl about her and turned up the wick of the lamp on the kitchen table.

Then she started to read. But soon she dozed off.

Susan woke to hear laughter coming from the parlor. "Whatever is the matter?" she thought. "Maybe they did get some cider from the cellar after all." She went out into the dark dining room to listen.

Through the open doors of the living room and parlor she could see, in the warm lamplight, four shadowy figures seated in rockers near the couch. Olive's face, which Joseph had wrapped from beneath the chin to the top of her head with a white handkerchief, was hardly visible in a dark corner of the couch.

It was Abe who was telling stories—telling jokes.

Susan was ashamed for him. *And just when it looked as though those two might be friends at last*, she mused, *he has to do something like this*.

127

She heard his chuckle before he spoke. "And after that twister took the church—every last board—and scattered it for ten miles, I guess, do you know what we found down in the hollow back of the cemetery?"

"I remember that story." The dark young man laughed, too. "But I heard the fellow that found it died of the D.T.s not long after."

"I swear it was a true story. I'm not a drinking man myself." The others laughed again. Even Joseph. "Well, not so's I can't get a straight picture. And I saw it, too."

"All right, Abe, let's hear what *you* saw," said the young man's father. "I never believed it, either."

"Well," Abe began, "pretty soon after the twister went on its way, snorting and threshing across the field, some of us started looking for hymnals and prayer books, in particular. Anything we thought we might be able to use again. We found some. Mostly they were drenched and torn up, though.

"But over there right in the middle of that swamp we found the church communion set. The linen cloth was still over the glasses, as neat as it had been on the side table at the altar. And not a drop of wine was spilled. Not a drop.

"I swear it. It's a true story."

Then Susan heard Joseph. "Well, anyway, it's a *good* story," he said, laughing. "Let me tell you now about the first time Olive heard a twister story."

Susan shut her ears. *How could they do it?*

There was Joseph, chatting and laughing, with Olive hardly cold right next to him. Telling tornado stories. And even funny stories about Olive.

She went back to the kitchen to make more coffee.

By the time she reached the parlor with a pot of coffee and plates with large pieces of spice cake on a big tray, the men were quiet again. Grief seemed to be gathering from the dark corners of the room along with the silence.

All at once she knew for the first time why mourners held wakes. People must need a chance to talk things out, to re-create just once more the world the dead had known, to share affection and common experiences.

When she set the tray down, she smiled at Joseph. "Did Olive ever tell you how happy she was when you decided to come along with us the day we got my piano from the station?" she asked. "She'd been feeling kind of put out, I thought. But then her eyes positively shone, Joseph, when you came out of the house and climbed up on that wagon in front of us. I'll never forget how happy she looked that morning."

The sadness lifted a little. Joseph smiled. "It *was* a good day, wasn't it?" he said. "We had a lot of good days, Olive and I."

CHAPTER 16

"NO, SUSAN, YOU MUST not take them away from their home," Joseph said. "I know you mean well, Susan, but I will not let my sons leave my sight." Though his ginger mustache and full beard covered his mouth, his tone of voice invited no response.

Susan was sitting at Olive's kitchen table, drinking coffee with Joseph and Abe, while Mrs. Gerber and her daughter and two other women from the neighborhood finished washing dishes on the far side of the big room. Susan looked to Abe for help. Maybe he could persuade Joseph to let her take the boys home with them for a few days. Ever since the services in the parlor were over, however—even during the long ride to the cemetery and back and while mourners lunched together and chatted quietly in the late afternoon heat—Abe had hardly spoken. The other farm families had left to do evening chores, and now Abe would have to leave, too.

Soon Joseph would be alone in the house. All alone, if the children went home with Susan.

Abe continued to stare morosely into his china cup. It was part of a set of hand-painted dishes that had been a wedding gift from their half-sister in Berlin. Tears came to Susan's eyes again when she remembered how Olive had loved those fragile, pretty dishes.

She sighed and turned back to Joseph. "Then I'll stay here with you tonight," she said. "However will you manage alone?"

Joseph straightened his back. He had not cried since the tornado struck two days before. Already the yard was cleared of debris. He had spent all his effort, night and day, planning and arranging for Olive's funeral. By the time of the wake on the second night, Abe's carefully planed and sanded and varnished pine coffin was ready. Susan had a vague notion that Joseph would rather have sent to the city for a satin-lined casket, but his allowing Abe to build one himself—since Abe knew nothing of city ways—made Susan feel good about the growing respect Joseph showed her husband. "No, Susan," Joseph said again, "Although I thank you kindly. Now let us say no more about it."

Abe finally stirred. "I'll get on home before long, Joseph," he said. "Susan will stay here and rouse the boys from their naps. Maybe she can get some pancakes stirred up for you to feed yourselves with in the morning." He took his felt hat from the rack by the door. "In the morning," he went on, "you can put some plans together. In such times as these, Joseph, things take a day or two to come clear."

131

Abe did no more than glance toward Susan before he left. But he had responded to her silent request. She stood by the door and watched him unhitch their horse from the post in order to take the buggy home. Then when she walked back across the fields later she would not have to care for the horse.

We do communicate, though, and he does *look out for me,* she told herself.

By the time Susan reached home, it was nearly dark. She lighted the oil lamp on the kitchen table. There was a note on a small piece of brown paper lying on the white linen cloth. "The chickens are fed. The eggs are in the cellar. I have taken care of the milk, too," it said.

Susan picked up the lamp and opened the bedroom door. Abe's black suit lay neatly on the bed and his good high-top shoes sat on the floor by the chifforobe. He must still be at the barn.

Although she watched at a kitchen window for several minutes she could see no light in the barn. Usually she was able to follow Abe's path from granary to cow stalls and from haymow to horse stable by the light from his lantern. Shadowy movements in the pasture beyond the barn told her he had put the cows out for the night.

Where is he? Maybe, she told herself, *on an unexpected errand to see a neighbor. Maybe to look at the condition of the ripening wheat.*

Susan sighed and turned toward the living room. Her mind was in turmoil and what she wanted most was an hour at her piano.

132

During the days since Olive died, Anna's chair had nearly leaped whenever Susan went into the room but tonight, although she stood over it and held the lamp high to catch any trace of movement, the chair was strangely quiet. The little faded blue cushion that often retained the contour of a body's having sat there— even after no one had used it—was plumped up, and the varnished pine gleamed in the lamplight.

Susan's piano gleamed, too. She set the lamp on one end of it and went to open a window to the hot August night. Immediately a big dusty moth flew in and began to flutter about the lampshade.

She began to play hymns they had sung at the services. Joseph had asked a choir director from the village to lead the mourners in Lutheran hymns. Some of them Susan knew, but there were low-church songs she had not heard before, too. Abe sang the slow, sentimental tunes along with the others, but Joseph and Susan did not. Her mother had always considered such peasant songs proper only for social gatherings where one necessarily had to mix with all kinds of people. Now Susan tried to pick out the melodies of some of the songs from memory.

When she opened a piece of sheet music to play a little Mozart, a mosquito sang past her ear, and then another. "If I don't shut them out they'll keep me up all night, swatting," she said as she rose to go to the window to close it.

It was very dark. The stars were out, but there was no light, not even a reflection from a bright field or from the stream by the marsh. The trees in the yard, too, were a part of the blur of black velvety heat. Only now and then a firefly flickered briefly. The countryside, though, was alive with chirps and bellowing cows and hooting owls. There was a smell of clover blossoms.

Just as she was about to close the window, Susan saw a wavering light far down the road toward the woods. It was coming along the route Abe had taken with her on that misty spring morning. No close neighbors lived in the woods, or beyond them. The light seemed to travel from side to side, stopping now and then.

Fear rose in her throat. Quickly she turned to look at the chair. It was quiet, just an ordinary little pine rocker.

She made herself turn again to the window. By now the light was closer. She could see that it came from a lantern carried by someone rather tall. Probably a man. Maybe just a neighbor walking on the road.

"I *am* skittish," Susan said aloud. "Why should a neighbor walking past our house upset me so much?" Then the lantern turned into their driveway.

With a sigh of relief Susan recognized the lantern and knew that Abe was home.

She took the lamp from the piano and ran to the kitchen door to greet him. "Wherever have you been, Abe?" she cried. "I tried not to worry, but I did, anyway!"

Abe blew out the lantern on the porch. Susan watched his face, gaunt and drawn in the faint light. Then he set an empty flowerpot on the porch. When he turned to come inside his eyes looked haunted and his mouth was grim. It was the face of Abe on the train

134

out of Chicago when he was remembering Anna, while their seat-companion coughed her life away.

Susan knew where he had been. He had taken a pot of her primroses to Anna's grave.

"Oh, Abe," she said, "I'm sorry I was cross with you." She paused. "We've both lost sisters now, you know."

Abe said nothing, but his look into her face was vacant, uncomprehending. He stumbled across the kitchen floor and into the bedroom. Susan heard him take off his shoes and then fall into bed.

She left the lamp on the kitchen table and went into the living room to close the window against the sudden chilly breeze. Against her will she turned to look at the chair.

It was rocking again, rhythmically, and the floorboards beneath it began to squeak. In the faint light she could see, too, that the cushion was crushed, as though bearing the weight of a body.

CHAPTER 17

Susan's mother sent a telegram: She was tending her increasingly feeble husband, but Laura would arrive within a week to help Joseph.

Joseph stayed sober until after Olive had been laid in the churchyard. But soon it was evident he was starting to drink again. One night Abe found him after he had put the children to bed, drinking whiskey at his kitchen table.

"It's just for a day or two, my boy," he'd said. "When the boys are with me at the barn or in the field, it's all right. But at night it's hard. Don't tell Susan, Abe. I'll be all right soon."

Abe did tell her, though, as soon as he got home. He talked about Joseph to her, but he never talked about Anna any more.

"I feel so—so lonely," she said to him. She looked wearily at her stark kitchen and her haunted—by now she believed it really was haunted—living room.

"But Susan, I'm here," Abe said, looking closely at her in the lamplight. "Olive's gone, but I am yours, too, you know."

She took his hand and held it against her cheek. *Are you? Are you completely mine?* she wondered.

Susan spent much of her time looking after the little boys during the next few days. Fredrick's mother helped her through the worst part of her grief. But by the end of the week Joseph was into a real binge.

He managed only to say, from time to time, "The boys must stay with me, Susan. I will hear no more about it." Even Abe was not able to reason with him.

Susan drove Joseph's buggy herself to the village to meet Laura's train. As Laura descended the steps, Susan saw that the little girl she had left in Milwaukee a few months earlier had become, at fourteen, a young woman. She had the same fair coloring as the other women in the family, and now she, too, pulled her hair severely back into a tawny bun.

Laura carried her small body, in its gray serge traveling suit and gray bonnet, with dignity. She walked rather than ran when she saw her sister. At Christmas she had run down to the family's candle-lit tree and giggled and shrieked over each new gift.

The sisters wept together while they sat in the buggy at the station, partly sheltered from curious eyes by an overhanging willow branch.

"I'll tell you about things on the way," said Susan. "There's so much to tell. I wanted to take the babies, but Joseph won't have it. He won't let them leave his house and I do have to care for things at home, too. It's the busiest time for farmers just now—and for farmer's wives—and there's so much I still have to learn as it is.''

Susan slapped the reins on the back of the horse. *And the worst news of all, I haven't told anybody,* she thought. *That's the main reason I can't do the work at both houses.*

For several weeks she had felt that ignoring her frequent morning nausea might make it go away somehow, and because she was busy, she was able to shove it to the back of her mind. But seeing Laura made her realize that now her responsibilities to Joseph would lighten, and her own home would be important again.

''*I* haven't lived on a farm, either, Susan. Is it hard to learn what to do?'' Laura asked.

Susan looked at her sister with concern. She had not thought about the misgivings the girl surely must have felt on the long ride across the state. After all, when Susan herself had come here, Abe had been her guide and protecter.

Susan laughed in what she hoped was a reassuring way. ''Oh, don't worry about taking care of the housework, Laura,'' she said. ''Fredrick Gerber, Joseph's hired man, has a wonderful mother, and she's taken over a lot of the chores. But Joseph needs a nurse for the babies. Mrs. Gerber will help you learn to tend to them, too.

''I'll be there as often as I can. Part of every day.''

Susan paused, trying to find the right words. ''What Joseph really needs,'' she went on, ''is somebody from the family to comfort him. That will be your hardest job.''

138

Soon enough she would have to discuss Joseph's drunkenness, but there was other information they could exchange on their first meeting.

They chatted easily while the horse made his way through the woods and past the grain fields and pasture land, raising hot dust from the bumpy road. Voracious mosquitoes greeted them when they passed through the swampy wooded areas, and a pungent smell of bog fires hung over fields everywhere.

"It's such *wild* country!" exclaimed Laura.

Susan glanced at her sister around the brim of her bonnet. The delighted smile might have been her own a few months earlier.

"Oh, Laura," she cried, "I'm so glad you've come. You're good for me! You make me remember things I must never forget." She resolved to herself, *It will work out. I'll make it work out. But I'll have to tell Abe soon.*

Susan stopped at Joseph's home long enough to unharness Joseph's horse and to watch Mrs. Gerber begin Laura's education. Mrs. Gerber was sitting on a stool by the kitchen table, peeling potatoes for supper. The woman's florid face beamed when she saw them. Her big print apron shook while she laughed her greeting.

"Well, now, another porcelain doll! My little *kinder* always begged for a doll with a por-ce-lain head when it was time for Father Christmas!"

She wiped her hands on her apron, picked up Laura's carpetbag, and led the way up the stairs.

"Now I've got a girl your age, too, already," Mrs. Gerber went on. "She's at home right now cooking for the men my mister's got helping with the wheat. My Martha can take over for me in the kitchen any day.''

Laura peered into the big walnut wardrobe in the spare bedroom where she would sleep. ''I surely don't have clothes enough to fill this,'' she exclaimed. ''I'll just move some of the boys' things in here.'' She was holding Karl, who was sucking his thumb, his solemn eyes inspecting her face. The baby was still napping in his crib in Joseph's room.

Mrs. Gerber laughed again. ''Your mother raised all of her girls the same way. I can see that! Right away you look things over and make plans. Just like your sisters.'' She paused. ''Well, maybe *you* can talk that man into letting the kiddies sleep in here with you. He won't have nobody near them when he's around the house, you know.''

Laura looked at Susan in surprise.

It was time to let Laura know about their problem, Susan thought. ''Joseph's—well, he's not himself these days, Laura,'' she began. ''I hope it will pass, but right now he's hard to deal with. He seems to think something might happen to the *boys,* too.

''And then,'' she paused, reluctant as always to discuss family matters in public, but realizing that after all the neighbors must know about Joseph's real problem, ''he does take more than enough hard cider. And even whiskey, too, now.''

''Oh, my, what would Mama say?'' Laura gasped, obviously as startled as Susan herself had been to hear this news from Abe. It seemed ages ago she had first learned Joseph was a drunkard.

140

"Is he—mean to other people then?" Laura asked, apparently concerned about the children, and probably about her own safety, too.

"No, thank heaven. He just sleeps a lot, and then he won't decide about things that have to be decided. And he cries. It won't always be easy for you, Laura, but I'll be close by, and so will Mrs. Gerber. All you have to do at first is to look out for the children and put some meals on the table. Olive had a fine garden."

"Joseph's a good man, my child," Mrs. Gerber offered, "but it's a bad time for him. A bad time."

Laura's eyes shone. "I can do it! Mama would want me to, since, I expect Susan told you, she can't be here herself."

Susan swallowed, her tears starting again. The tears were for her little sister this time.

On the way back to her own home late that afternoon Susan walked along the fence rows, picking enough blackberries to fill her apron. Each day she picked berries, and at night she made jam or prepared them for drying. Some of the berries she would take back for Joseph's family the next morning.

Mrs. Gerber advised her, and she remembered her mother's teaching, and she continued to learn to keep house in a way more primitive than she could have imagined back in Milwaukee.

When she reached home she carried wood, fed the chickens, gathered the eggs, polished the lamp chimneys, and by the time Abe came in from cutting wheat, she had prepared boiled potatoes and scrambled eggs. There were new radishes from the garden, and berries.

Susan worried about the supper. She still often cooked meals that would easily satisfy the appetite of an elderly urban male who exercised by handling the reins of horses harnessed to a buggy, rather than for a vigorous young farmer with a ravenous appetite.

Susan stepped outside to chat with Abe while he washed up on a bench next to the back door. The sun had just dropped below the horizon.

"Laura has grown up," she told him with a smile. "I think she'll take over her new job like a veteran."

"All of you are alike." He chuckled, taking off his shoes and putting on the slippers she had ready for him. "You really get folks into line! Look what you've done to me already, making me take off my shoes and mind my manners at the table, too. And even give up my chewing tobacco. Next thing you know I won't be able to have my pipe any more, either. But I figure it'll be a *long* time before I do that!"

"Do you know, that's what Mrs. Gerber said, that we are—or were—all alike? I think *she* meant it as a compliment, though, when she said it."

Abe looked at her with an amused grin. "I won't fall into *that* trap."

Susan decided she would take advantage of his good mood. While she started to put the food on the table, she said, "You know, I figure a woman has to kind of—well, prepare a nest—before she puts babies into it."

She concentrated her attention on lighting the new oil lamp her mother had sent in the trunk from home. The wick flared briefly and then became steady when she put the chimney over it. Out of the corner of her eye she saw Abe's look of surprise. And then of pleasure.

As usual, his comment came slowly. "By George, that's good news, Susan." He paused. "It *is* news now, isn't it?"

His happiness was infectious. She somehow had to respond to it.

"Yes," she said quietly, dropping into a chair across from him, "it *is* news, and I guess I'm lucky to be feeling so well, especially with the way things have been for all of us lately."

He reached across the table and took her hand in both of his. "I'm a lucky man, too, Susan," he said.

Then he folded his hands and bowed his head. In addition to the traditional Lutheran prayer before meals he now added, *"Father in Heaven, we thank Thee for Thy special blessing on this household. Amen."*

"Amen." breathed Susan, because she felt he expected her to.

CHAPTER 18

DURING THE NIGHT Susan thought she heard thunder. She remembered she had not closed the door to the shed where the chickens slept and where they laid eggs in the boxlike nests Abe had built for them next to their roosting poles. The bottom half of the doorway was covered to keep out foxes and raccoons, but because of the summer heat Susan had left the top partially open.

A heavy rainstorm, her sleepy brain told her, *will soak the fresh straw in the shed.* She waited for a few moments, drowsing. Then the thunder sounded closer.

She quietly slid out of bed and put on a light shawl and her shoes.

The air was cool in the yard, and rich with smells of clover and cows and blossoming summer weeds. An old moon was rising, giving an orange glow to trees and fields. For a little while Susan sat on the back porch and watched a bank of storm clouds pass from the west toward the north. Heat lightning played across the sky, but it looked as though the rain would not reach their farm. She was relieved. Abe's wheat needed a few days to dry in the sun before it could be threshed.

As Susan rose to go back into the house, she became aware of a flash of movement along the road near the porch off the living room. But she had heard no sound of footsteps in the still air.

She went down the porch steps and around to the corner of the house, straining her eyes in the darkness.

On the narrow dirt road a slight figure in a black dress seemed to float rather than walk from the direction of the woods toward Susan's front door. The woman's face was shadowed. When she came nearer, Susan saw that a dark head scarf was pulled far down over her forehead, hiding her features.

Susan stopped short of rounding the corner for a moment, not wanting to startle the stranger. She waited for a while longer, but saw nothing more. Could the woman still be standing in front of the house? Or had she turned back toward the woods? Susan was curious but unalarmed when she stepped around the corner, even though she knew she would now be in plain sight of the stranger in the light of the rising moon.

For the first time she felt a small stir of apprehension rising in her throat.

There was no one in front of the house or on the road. Susan looked carefully in both directions. She even went out into the road and peered across the fields.

There was no movement anywhere and no sound of retreating footsteps. The only sounds were an owl's hooting in the elm tree next to the house and the occasional bawling of a cow in the pasture.

Susan's feet seemed to crunch loudly on the spot of gravel outside her back porch and in her mind, her leather shoes thundered across the porch.

Then, when she passed the open door to the living room, she saw the figure again. It was sitting in Anna's rocking chair.

The chair rocked with its usual slow rhythm and the floorboards beneath it creaked.

Susan's heart began to pound and her vision blurred, but she made a sudden decision to have it out with whatever had been troubling her before she became too frightened to act. She rushed into the room.

Then she stopped. The figure was gone, although the rocker was still gently rocking. The living room, though, seemed strangely empty.

Although the little pine rocker was still there, her piano had disappeared.

Susan screamed until she was exhausted. Her mouth was wide open, but no sound came out. Her dry throat made it hard to swallow. Still gasping for breath, somehow she dragged herself to her bed and fell into it. Abe did not stir. She lost consciousness.

By morning light, her living room looked the same way it had at bedtime the night before. Abe, happy with last evening's news of his impending fatherhood, asked if she had slept well.

"I did," he said. His slow smile spread across his

face and lighted his eyes. "I woke up once or twice," he went on. "The moonlight came in our window, Susan, and I could see you were sleeping like a baby—with a smile on your face that told me how pleased you really are about being in the family way." He pulled on his jacket, ready to go to the barn in the early morning chill.

Susan closed her eyes and sighed deeply. She put her head against his shoulder. The rough cloth, with its faint smell of the fields, was comforting. *It was only a nightmare*, she told herself.

But when she went into the kitchen, she found her shoes and her shawl on the floor next to the living room door.

CHAPTER 19

In spite of her disappointment when she remembered all the plans she had made, Susan found she could not deny the new life inside her. The baby began to assume a personality for her, and she talked to it while she weeded the garden.

The baby still had no sex, no potential beyond the stark fact of its existence. But there was no one else to talk to. The dog stayed with Abe in the fields. He was not a house dog. And although she was determined to keep the rocking chair out of her thoughts, it kept creeping back. To keep Anna away she sang a lot, or she talked aloud about her work. Now she talked to the baby.

"I'll pull these carrots in the fall," she murmured, "and I'll bury them in leaves or sawdust in the cellar, and by next spring I'll mash them up so you can eat some of them."

Susan finally convinced herself that her experience

during the hour of the distant storm had been only a nightmare. Obviously she had walked in her sleep, too, leaving her shawl and shoes in the kitchen. The life inside her gave her a new strength and a new wisdom.

For most of the time she was able to close her mind to the vision of the dark woman on the road.

One afternoon she seated herself defiantly in Anna's rocking chair—even though the memory that it had been Olive's favorite, too, crossed her mind. She sewed the seams of her curtains while she rocked, and she whispered, "Next year I'll rock you to sleep in this chair. And your grandma will visit, and she'll rock you, too."

Sooner or later, she told herself, Anna would have to give up her hold on the chair, and on their lives, now that a new generation was about to enter the barn-house. And she was thankful for the fact that the moans that had terrified her the first night never sounded through the rooms again. The chair, in fact, had not moved since the night of Olive's funeral—if indeed, it *had* moved then.

Abe was spending much of his time away from home, since he helped neighbors with their threshing. In another week or so it would be her turn to cook for a dozen men and boys when the threshing machine came to their farm, but now she had an hour to spare before she must feed the chickens and gather eggs. She decided to visit Laura.

"I got a letter from Mama," Laura told her. "Fredrick went to the village to have a horse shod, and he brought the letter back. Mama says Papa won't eat any more. She wants you to come home to see him, but she doesn't want to ask you because she knows you are needed here.

"I think she's lonesome for you, Susan. Aunt Elviry comes in to help now and then, but the only person living with her now—except for Papa—is a new hired girl Mama is just starting to train. I guess it's hard for her to get used to an empty house, when there was always so much going on all the time with their business acquaintances—even after most of us children were away."

For a moment Laura looked downcast. Then a smile from the baby she was rocking in his cradle restored her high spirits. "Oh, well," she said, "maybe the next letter will have better news."

Laura had blossomed in her work. She loved the children, and they clung to her skirts, gazing at her with adoring eyes. Joseph was gentle with her, and he hid his drinking so cleverly he never offended her. Because she was innocent Laura was unaware of sure signs of his descent into drunkenness.

Susan felt sad about her mother's burden, but her life with her parents now seemed a hundred years behind her. "I wonder if Karl would ever think of coming home to help out for a little while. After all, the rest of us can't leave what we're doing," she mused almost to herself as she began to sort and fold the children's clothes Laura had heaped on the kitchen table. The big kitchen was cool in spite of the heavy summer heat outside, and Susan was reluctant to start back across the fields while the sun was still high.

"Whatever are you saying?" Laura laughed. "Karl

has his *studies* to attend to. Papa would never let *him* come home!''

"I've been thinking," Susan began slowly, "why shouldn't *you* be going off to the Old Country to study? Or why didn't I?''

"Goodness," cried her sister, "you *have* been away from Papa a long time! Do you talk to Abe like that?''

Susan was startled by that thought. "No, as a matter of fact, I guess I haven't. Not very much, anyway.'' She paused. "But I will! In due time, I will. If this is a girl I'm carrying, and she wants to go to Berlin to study, she'll go! Laura, I wonder how much Mama made me feel the way I do. She'd never speak up for me about this kind of thing, but she's pretty independent. She advises Papa in lots of his deals. And she makes some of her own, too.''

Laura looked at her curiously. "Susan, didn't— well, it was hard for us to tell from her letters—didn't Olive have a happy life here? I've had a terrible thought since I've been here in this house. Did Olive really die from getting hit by lightning during a tornado? Was there something you couldn't tell Mama?''

For a moment Susan was speechless. "What did she write to you?''

"Nothing, really, except she sounded miserable. Mama took to reading her letters to me lately, and then we would both cry. There would be things like 'These peasants have no manners. How can I rear my children in this wild country?' And one time she wrote, 'Joseph's illness depresses me. He becomes more remote from me and from the children. If he takes to his bed, whatever will I do?' ''

151

"Did she mention Abe or me? We tried to help."

"Oh, yes, she did. You, especially."

Susan sighed. "She thought Abe was just another 'peasant.' I couldn't stand that." She paused. "I wish I'd been kinder, though. I didn't know how hard it was for her."

She saw that Laura was still waiting for an answer to her question. "No, no, the lightning killed Olive. Somehow—Abe can't figure out how—the baby was thrown free. I was with her, just the way I told you on the drive home from the train.

"But now that I've had time to think about it all, I wonder if Olive would have lived to see her children grow up at that. Maybe the lightning was a welcome messenger for her."

"Susan!" cried Laura. "What has happened to you? You were the last one to be superstitious! Mama said it's not unusual for a woman with too much work to do to feel the way Olive did, especially if she has babies too fast. But we worried about her neighbors around here, too, with their rough manners and bad habits. And what she said was true, Susan. It was true."

Susan was hardly listening. *Was* she becoming superstitious? Was it possible the empty house, with its unsolved mysteries that she could not discuss with Abe, and the long lonely days, were beginning to work their way with her?

As she walked home she resolved to invite the congregation in for a hymn sing as soon as the threshing was done.

If the weather held, in another week the grain would

be in bins in the barn or on its way to market. Later, with both oats and wheat out of the way, the farmers would not be quite so busy as they had been. Abe even had talked about taking her and Laura to the county fair.

But first she would have her hymn sing. She liked the neighbors she had met, in spite of Olive's feeling about them, and she wanted to know them better.

The next few days were the most exhausting Susan had ever known. In spite of Mrs. Gerber's help and advice, cooking for and serving the dozen men who came to feed the cut wheat into the threshing machine and drive teams of horses and shovel the grain and bag it made for long days of constant, heavy work.

Abe brought up hard cider from kegs in the cellar and took jugs of it to the field. Then he put the jugs on the tablecloth Susan had placed on planks over sawhorses under a tree. The men sat on benches to eat potatoes and beans and ham. They drank and joked and shouted. Afterward the older ones napped briefly, stretched out on the grass, while the boys played horseshoes. Summer heat shimmered over the stubble in the field beyond the barn and katydids sang in the long dry grass. Susan sat for a few minutes at the kitchen table with a china cup half-filled with strong coffee from the bottom of a big blue enamel coffeepot.

Then the men went back to work, and Susan washed dishes and began to prepare the next meal. She washed and ironed towels and tablecloths and baked extra bread and churned extra butter. Laura, she had decided, would only be in the way and the boys would be underfoot, so she had not asked her to come. Now she almost wished she had. Even though Laura would have been appalled by the men's manners and jokes, her sister's cheerful disposition might have lifted her spirits while she wrestled with confusion and inexperience during the long, hot afternoon.

And Abe was no help at all. Except for a brief "Everything all right?" and a perfunctory "Anything I can do?" he seldom had time to come near the house. Without a son or a hired man, he had his hands full keeping up with his own responsibilities.

At last, after the threshing rig had left, they sat down together in the lamplight at the kitchen table, and Abe totaled up his profits. He wrote with his pencil stub on a piece of wrapping paper while Susan darned socks stretched over a gourd.

"Susan, so far it's been a good year." Abe leaned back and lit his pipe with a sliver of wood he had put into the glowing ashes of the range. "It looks as though we can feed our stock and we can feed ourselves, too—all three of us. If we have extra money after the corn crop when we've saved enough out for taxes and we're through paying on the mortgage for this quarter," he paused and smiled, "what should we do with the money left over?"

For the first time Susan felt as though he was including her as a partner, not as a novice whose work was still on approval.

"Oh, Abe," she said, "we need a cistern under the house, with a pump in the kitchen, like I had at home. Then a well near the back door, with a windmill over it, like Joseph has. After that—"

154

"Whoa! Susan, we didn't buy out the bank! We only made a reasonable profit!"

He was laughing, but she felt angry. Now he was not treating her like a partner, but like a child he had to indulge. She closed her mouth tightly so she would not say something she would surely be sorry for later, but she abruptly put down her darning and strode into the warm night.

She was so weary.

Then as she began to walk down the dusty road she started to realize she had answered Abe the way a child would—a child, demanding toys for Christmas.

Abe, she knew, had his own priorities—buying new pasture land, for one thing. And Abe was eternally an adult, not ever having experienced childhood. All at once she could see that Abe's attitude bore no resemblance to her father's paternalism she had come to resent so bitterly.

It was her father she had been fighting tonight in her kitchen, not her husband.

She turned around slowly and walked back.

Once inside, Susan looked down into Abe's patient, perplexed face, and then she stooped over and kissed him lightly on the mouth. "I'm back," she said. "I'm back for good."

The next morning, after Abe had taken a load of wheat to the mill in the village to be ground, Susan began to feel most unusual. She stretched and yawned, and then she stretched again. Soon her muscles started to ache. Before long, stretching failed to relieve her growing discomfort.

Within a few minutes she found that, in spite of the hot summer sun outside, she was shaking with cold. She wrapped a quilt around her shoulders and dragged herself to the living room sofa. She tried to find a position she could stand for more than an instant. Her teeth chattered, but cold sweat poured from her forehead.

Oh, Abe, she prayed, *come home. O, Dear God, what can be wrong with me? O, God, don't let it hurt my baby!* She rolled about, moaning.

By the time Abe found her, the chills had disappeared, but her temperature had begun to rise. She was throwing off the quilt and tearing at the button on her collar.

"Water! Water!" she called to Abe when he came in the door. He looked briefly at her and then he ran to the water bucket in the kitchen. He dipped a towel into a basin of cool water and knelt down beside her, soothing her hot face and her wrists.

"Oh, Abe, whatever is the matter with me?" she wept.

"It's only the ague, Susan," he replied calmly, but his eyes on her face showed his concern. "Everybody gets the ague. It'll be gone in a little while, and then you'll feel good again, I promise you."

"Will it hurt the baby?" Her lips were parched, and she choked when she tried to talk.

"If it hurt babies before they came into the world, I guess we wouldn't have any babies around here." He smiled sadly. "We all get it, sooner or later. It comes in summer, mostly."

He wrung out the towel over the washbasin and

dipped it again into the water. "If you grow up here, you build up a kind of defense against it, I guess. Not many folks die from the ague, Susan, but it's mighty miserable while it lasts."

Abe was right. As soon as the fever passed, she felt exceptionally well. Better than she had felt for a long time.

But the experience had taken its toll.

I wonder what other things might have happened to Olive to make her come to such a sad state, thought Susan that night while Abe snored softly beside her. *In time I may know some of those, too.*

CHAPTER 20

THAT SUNDAY NIGHT Susan and Abe had their hymn sing. Susan polished the chimneys of their best kerosene lamps until they sparkled and then set them on the table and on the piano in the living room. They moved their kitchen chairs and a small rocker from the bedroom to line the walls. An afternoon storm had cleared the muggy air, but moths collected around lamp chimneys as soon as it began to get dark.

The Gerbers, with their children and an aged grandmother, came in a buggy, but Joseph and Laura walked across the fields, carrying the two boys. Laura put the baby to bed. Several men Susan had met at the train station and a woman she once chatted with at the dry goods store arrived with their families and their hired hands. The hired men, in clean but carefully mended coats and trousers, sat on the pine-plank front porch until it was time to come inside and stand near the door. They laughed and swapped stories in Low German as the night closed in.

Jake Gross, who had helped unload her piano, brought a giggling blond girl friend. Susan's critical eye noted the small bustle on the girl's white lawn dress. Women in Milwaukee had stopped wearing bustles like that five years earlier. Laura, Susan noticed, was trying to get perspective on the country atmosphere around her, too.

The brothers who owned the threshing rig, bachelors from the village, rode out with summer apples for everyone. Susan had made stollen and she would serve coffee. Swabish and Bavarian dialects flew about the hot little room, but nobody chewed tobacco.

Each guest took a turn choosing a hymn. Susan had asked for a song book from the minister at the small Evangelical church in the village soon after her piano arrived, and she was ready to play any gospel song they might want to sing. The Lutheran hymns she had grown up with seemed austere compared with these jingling tunes, but her neighbors sang with the same enthusiasm she remembered from congregations at home.

After the hymns, one of the men struck up a popular song in German, and then the women and children joined in. Her living room echoed with music, while women fanned themselves and children swatted mosquitoes.

When Susan came back from the kitchen with plates of stollen and the apples, an ancient grandmother had begun a ghost story. She was sitting in Anna's chair, rocking slowly.

The old woman's watery blue eyes were sunk deep in wrinkles, but they sparkled in the lamplight.

"My aunt," she was saying, "could make a table dance. And she taught me the trick. First off, though, there's got to be a willing spirit in the house.

"Most spirits ain't evil things, you know. Not bad things at all. They just don't care much. They ain't willing nor unwilling. It's *us* that causes all the trouble with spirits. The spirits is only *there*. That's all." She nodded to herself over her wise observation. Then she went on.

"Abe, your house is haunted. Why don't you bring that little table over there in the corner to the middle of the room? I'd kind of like to try my hand at it again. Let's us just see if your haunt is a willing one."

Abe seemed amused. "What makes you think this house is haunted, Granny Hosmer?"

"Everybody knows about poor Mr. O'Neill's body in the cellar," she said, "trying to get itself Christian buried. And about that horse, too, that horse of his that keeps whinnying on winter nights down to the swamp where it threw him." The old woman was looking intently at Abe.

"Well, I've lived here a long time now, Granny," he said, "and I don't like to disappoint you, but I've never seen any ghosts."

"I hear your sister Anna did, though," she murmured slyly, nodding her white head as if to herself.

Abe stopped smiling. The room was suddenly still.

"Now, now, Granny," whispered her daughter.

Finally he spoke. "Do you know, at one time Anna and I did hear some sounds? They seemed to come

160

from the loft, where I used to sleep, but they were back in a far corner.''

Laura could not restrain herself. ''Whatever did you find?'' she asked.

''Sensible girl.'' Abe's slow smile broke across his face. ''When I looked around I found a loose board that sounded kind of like a moan when the wind blew in from the east, before a rain. After I nailed that board down, though, we never heard those sounds again.''

Susan whispered hoarsely, ''Never?''

''Never.'' He paused. ''But then, Susan, the day after you and I moved in here, I went up to the loft to hunt for something, and it looked as though maybe you had moved a trunk when you were cleaning, and I guess you must have loosened that board. So I nailed it back in place.'' He smiled again. ''That's the only ghost I ever knew about, Granny. But I'll bring that table out here for you, anyway, if you'd like to try to make it dance!''

Susan rose and went into the kitchen. She leaned against the wall, sighing deeply. Now she remembered that Olive had gone up to the loft that first day, and then she'd heard her sister moving things about during her tour of inspection.

And she had a distinct memory of a rising east wind that same night, before the rain started.

So much for peasant superstitions, she mused. *There's always a sensible answer. There always is.*

A little later, when some of the ghost stories had sent proper chills along their spines, and the table had *not* danced, Abe asked that they all kneel for a prayer before leaving for home. Susan silently gave thanks—for her piano, for Granny Hosmer, and for Abe, who had finally cleared up some of the mystery she had been trying to push to the back of her mind. Now she could look forward with pleasure to her solitary winter evenings while Abe was busy with chores in the barn, and not with a dread of hearing those awful moans again. That dread had been growing as the months passed, in spite of her vow to ignore it.

But the chair still rocked. Recently it had begun to rock rapidly whenever she looked into the living room. Susan no longer sat in it.

And she had not yet been able to talk with Abe about getting rid of a chair that had such personal memories for him.

"Abe, will you carry those cups out here for me?" Susan called from the kitchen after the last buggy had pulled away. Abe was standing in the doorway watching summer clouds drifting across the moon. Probably he was planning Monday's work. Crickets and frogs chorused from swampy fields beyond the woods.

"You do beat the devil, making me take on women's work," he said, bringing the dishes. He seemed happy and ready to chat. "How do you like our 'wild' neighbors now? Did they have bad manners?"

"Abe, it was a fine evening!" She paused, her mood changing. "I've never been around people who believe in ghosts, though. Granny Hosmer actually thought she could make that table dance! I'm not sure children should hear tales like that."

"I grew up with stories like those." He smiled at her, his smile a little teasing above the warm light of the lamp in his hand. "Maybe tables *do* dance, sometimes."

Susan stopped stacking the dishes. "Abe! I can't believe my ears!"

"Do you know, Susan," he went on, "my teacher in high school liked to quote pretty lines Shakespeare wrote, especially from that *Hamlet* I have on the shelf in the living room. I say them over to myself—and to the trees—when I follow a horse out in the fields. I'm particularly partial to those words about more things in heaven and earth than we can dream of. Did you study Shakespeare's plays when you went to your school in Milwaukee?"

"No. Goethe and Martin Luther. A little Heine. I like his kind of poetry. I love poetry when it's set to music." She paused. "But for me that doesn't have anything to do with superstition—that 'between heaven and earth.'"

Then she remembered the most important thing she wanted to talk about. "But Abe," she said, beginning to wash the china dishes her mother had sent, "you did set my mind at rest. I never could bring myself to tell you about the noise I heard in the loft that first night. It was the time you came in and found I had lights all over the house. I was scared, I'll have to admit it. Now I know Olive must have moved the trunk and loosened the board that made the noise while she was up there that morning. I'm so relieved." She smiled at him. "It's one more superstition killed, isn't it? Everything has an explanation, and we always find it out—sooner or later. Mama and Papa believed that, of course, and so did my teachers at the Lutheran school."

163

"I'm not sure, Susan. I sometimes think a little mystery isn't a bad thing." He set the last kitchen chair back next to the table, now covered with a white linen cloth. He continued, in what seemed to her a deliberately casual voice, "Has anything else bothered you since you came to live here? Anything else like that?"

Susan looked at him sharply. He was on his way into the living room to take the Bible down for their nightly reading.

"Well, I've been holding off on this, too, Abe, because it seems like such a foolish thing," she began slowly. "Could there be some loose boards in the living room floor? Wherever I move that small rocker, it still—"

She saw him stop suddenly, his hand in the air, as he reached up for the heavy book. Then he seemed to force his hand to complete the action, but he did not turn around.

"Oh, Abe, you've seen it, too! It rocks by itself, doesn't it? There must be some explanation, though, like with the sounds in the loft, don't you think?"

Abe turned around, his dark eyes troubled. "I often felt like she was in the room with me. Especially the living room. I don't know why. It always seemed kind of—comforting. But that was before you came to live here. I like to think she's still here, Susan."

Susan looked at him, searching for words. She took a deep breath. "Maybe, Abe," she said, "we've both been, well, troubled. And then our imaginations started working. That sometimes happens, you know, when people are nervous or—or troubled."

"In your kind of life, Susan, the way you were raised, folks think they can find answers for everything." He seemed to strive for proper words, too. "But here in the country nobody ever knows what the next day will bring. Some things we have to admit we can't explain."

She did not want to hurt him, or to make him think she felt superior to him. "Abe," she began slowly, *"This* is my life now, too. But let me help you understand *my* way of looking at things. You might get to like some parts of my way, you know, if you try them out."

Abe said nothing. But then he smiled. "Susan, do you remember what you asked me the other day when you had the ague? 'Will it hurt the baby?' That's the first time you seemed to care about the baby. Did you know that?"

So he had noticed her lack of enthusiasm for her pregnancy. She might as well be honest. "I told you all along I wanted to wait awhile, Abe. Until we had more to offer a family. But I found out how I really felt that day, too. And now things will be different. I'm not even going to the county fair with you. You can take Laura and the boys. That bumpy road would do me no good, I expect."

"Then I won't go either this year. Joseph or Fredrick can tell me about the new machines and about who won prizes." His dark eyes shone. "Next year we'll all go together."

Susan settled down against her pillow when Abe sat in their bedroom rocker and prepared to read his usual chapter in the Bible. She watched him as he pondered a moment over the empty lines in the center—waiting for their first entry.

The struggle between his wife and his sister would go on. And now Susan knew Abe was aware of the struggle, too.

But I'm going to win, she thought. Even when she had moved the little chair out to the yard one day, though, it went on moving slightly—but rhythmically—in the still air.

Susan decided the rocker would have to meet with an accident.

When at last she went to sleep, she was still making and discarding plans for the accident.

CHAPTER 21

"ABE AND I," Susan wrote her mother, "have begun to entertain our neighbors. I am anxious for you to meet them. I know you and Mrs. Gerber will like each other. Her parents came from Swabia fifty years ago, but she sends her children to a Lutheran school." She crossed out "Pa and Ma." Already she was beginning to talk like people around her.

Most of the Evangelicals and Catholics send theirs to the public school. Our grain crops gave an excellent yield, and Abe says this is a good year for corn, because it has been hot. There will be apples for cider and for drying. My garden has already supplied me with three crocks of pickles, and I made sauerkraut today.

She went on to wish her father a return to health and to reassure her mother about Laura's good work and constant high spirits.

By the time Laura has to return for school, I am sure she will have seen Joseph through the worst of his bereavement. I hope by then he will let me have the boys here. Joseph continues to be poorly, though, and soon he may not be able to care for his little ones.

Abe's Mr. Spencer, who reared him, has a young niece whose parents were killed at the time of the tornado, and we are thinking of asking her to come here to live and to help me with the children. Mr. Spencer died several years ago. I believe there is an older boy, too, in the family, and we think he might agree to help Abe with the work in the fields. That is the way Abe grew up, you know, and I think he feels he wants to help the Spencers if he can. We were told the youngsters would be separated, since they are charity cases. I really look forward to having them with us.

Then Abe can buy more land to work, too. I wish you could see how his neighbors depend on him already, even though he is younger than most of them. He has an education, you know, and he is clever, too, Mama.

Susan

Susan hummed to herself as she walked across the wheat stubble with her letter. The katydids chattered all about her. Since it was Saturday, she knew Fredrick would ride into the village to visit the tavern in the evening, and he could leave her letter to be mailed. Now Abe, with a baby on the way and other young people coming to live in the house, too, would have a good reason to begin finishing the loft as soon as his heavy work was over in the fall. And the Spencer boy could milk cows and feed pigs and horses for Abe. They would have a *household*. Her circle was expanding in a most pleasant way.

But she found Laura in tears. Since the first harvest was in, Joseph had lost all interest in the farm again.

168

He had taken to lying on the dining room couch much of the day. Usually he got up to eat at noon, but by evening he was often too intoxicated to come to the table. He rambled on about going back to Prussia to die.

"Susan," Laura wept, "I've tried to keep my trouble to myself, the way Mama would want me to. But I'm so tired of cleaning those old smelly milk and cream cans and washing clothes and getting meals. I thought maybe Joseph would be better by now. He isn't, though, Susan. He's getting worse."

"Maybe you could talk to him about plans for the boys. Or about the crops," Susan suggested.

"That's another problem. Fredrick has to decide what to do about selling off wheat, and keeping some of it. Joseph just goes on putting him off, but Fredrick doesn't dare ask his father or Abe. You know how Joseph feels about outsiders, especially peasants. And then there are the boys. There are things I have to know I don't think you know about, either."

"Can't you call on Mrs. Gerber?"

"She's busy putting up fruit and vegetables for winter. And that's another thing. Joseph won't have anything to eat next winter except potatoes. I haven't put anything up. What's going to happen to him?"

Susan felt guilty about her earlier good spirits. She should have kept a closer watch over Olive's household, but Laura had always smiled and pretended everything was fine. Susan remembered her sister was, after all, only fourteen.

"I wish you'd told me before this how bad Joseph is," she said quietly. Laura's face puckered up again, so she added quickly, "But I know you are doing your best."

Susan was glad she had finished her letter earlier. Their mother should hear just good news since she was so far away, and she would only fret helplessly over more bad news.

"Don't cry," said Susan with a sigh. "I'll get Abe to talk to Joseph. I'm sure things will work out." She sat on a stool next to the kitchen table and began to peel potatoes for supper. Since her body had started to thicken, she found it easier than before to rest as often as she could.

"And Karl misses Olive," Laura went on, dropping down across from her sister. "He cries in his sleep, even more than he did at first. The little one has some kind of summer complaint, too, probably from all those plums Fredrick gave him.

"Susan, I'm not sure I want any children of my own. I probably shouldn't say it, with you in the family way, but that's how I feel now." She almost whispered, "Maybe Olive did, too."

"I know," agreed Susan. "Some people can't stand the lonely times and the hard work, I guess. I think Olive and Joseph didn't neighbor enough, myself." She paused. "Wouldn't you like to neighbor with Fredrick's sister Martha a little?"

"Susan, you're beginning to talk just like these peasants. Did you know that? The Gerbers are pleasant people, but, well—"

For a moment Susan was offended, and she almost became defensive about Abe and their neighbors. Then her old positive outlook returned. "But they

170

survive—people like the Gerbers! I'm going to keep my standards and my strength, too. You just wait and see!''

For a moment Laura smiled again. "I'm anxious to tell Mama what you're doing. She probably won't say anything. You can bet she'll be proud of you, though." Laura looked with distaste at the clothes basket next to the door, but then she picked it up and strolled out toward the line filled with diapers blowing in the late afternoon breeze.

By the time Susan had reached home she felt she was in for another bout with the ague. It was not as frightening as the first time because she knew what would happen. Before she could get a quilt, though, she had begun to shake with chills. She lay on the red lap robe Adolph had given them and pulled it around her.

It would be an hour before Abe might come to the house, so she would have to see herself through the worst part alone. The violence of this attack at first annoyed her, and then she became alarmed. Her body ached. She rolled about on the couch, moaning, and once she bit her lip to keep from screaming.

As the living room darkened with approaching dusk, the chills finally began to ease. Susan raised her damp head from the pillow—already she was feeling the onset of fever—and saw the rocker. Somehow in her delirium it seemed right, and even comforting, to watch the chair move rhythmically back and forth, back and forth.

"Anna," she gasped, "are you calling me? Or is it

171

Olive this time? Do you both want me with you?"

She closed her eyes as the pains subsided for a moment. It would be so peaceful, so good, to leave this hard earth.

Then the fever attacked anew, and she threw herself about, sinking her teeth into the edge of Adolph's carriage blanket. She had to do something, anything, to get relief.

The chair rocked merrily, faster and faster, mocking her misery. The floorboards beneath it seemed to thunder in her ears. Suddenly she made a wild leap, crashing to the floor, determined to silence them forever.

When Abe reached her, Susan was still lying on the floor. He soothed her forehead with a wet towel the way he had before.

"This time it was too much," she wept. "I hurt myself. I threw myself against Anna's chair. It wouldn't stop rocking, Abe. It just wouldn't stop."

Then Abe lifted the carriage robe and he saw all the blood. "Oh, Susan, Susan," he sobbed.

She was aware of his arms tight around her before she fainted again.

Susan remembered only snatches of time during that night. Between the pain and the constant sound of creaking floorboards beneath that chair out in the living room, she was aware of people coming and going—Mrs. Gerber, Laura, Dr. Hosmer, Joseph, and Abe—whose anxious face encompassed all the other floating faces.

She tried to tell Abe that Anna was out there rocking. Rocking and laughing at her. But the words could not reach her parched lips.

She awoke finally to sunlight, blinding August sunlight. She turned her eyes away from it, though, and closed them again.

The wild swampy country had beaten her.

Worse than that, Anna had beaten her.

Maybe people from outside, Susan concluded wearily, were not strong enough to survive in this harsh, unsettling world. Only the heartier pioneers had stayed (and had even thrived) over the years. But many of them seemed to allow spooks—here she was using a vulgar word again—a place in their lives.

She recalled, too, the numerous tiny tombstones in each family plot in the cemetery next to the frame church in the village—and the names of all those young women on tombstones.

But it was not just the women and babies who died young here. When they had found a tombstone with Abe's family name on it one day, he blurted out a surprised, "But my uncle was only twenty-eight years old! He was the family drunkard, you know, and he looked like an old man to me the time I saw him when I was a little tad. Pa said his brother's crops failed and his cattle died, and he just didn't have a way with farming."

Abe came to the bedroom door and looked in for a second time. Susan knew she must do something, but she could not remember what. She felt weak, weaker than she had ever felt before, and incapable of coping with any demand on her energy. She fell asleep again.

Late in the day when she awoke, Mrs. Gerber's big

flowered apron came into focus beside her bed. Their neighbor had settled her heavy body into the small bedroom rocker next to the bed. The little chair creaked under her weight. "There, there, child," she was saying. "Now you've had a good, healthful rest. It's the best thing a woman can do at a time like this. I got some fine buttermilk here for you to drink now, Mrs. Hesse. I put it in one of your mama's best china cups. Let me lift your head already, child."

The buttermilk did help her to wake up and she became aware of her pain again. But the world had begun to assume its proper proportions, and she suddenly wanted to talk to Abe, to comfort him. For now she knew those lines in the Bible would remain blank.

She could find no words, though, for Abe.

CHAPTER 22

AT THE END OF A WEEK Dr. Hosmer stopped by to examine Susan for the last time. She was sitting up on the couch in the living room with a pillow at her back and Adolph's red lap robe wrapped about her.

Because of the August heat, Dr. Hosmer had taken off his suit coat and he sat in Abe's rocker, which he had drawn up next to Susan. His vest and rumpled white shirt smelled faintly of male sweat.

"I believe now there's no reason you can't have a family, Mrs. Hesse," the doctor boomed, his great bass voice filling the room, "but you are going to have to wait awhile. Abe might just have lost you this time, my child. He might just have lost you."

Abe was standing by the window. "It's only Susan that matters, Doc," he said quietly.

Susan had developed such a deep depression that neither the doctor's tentative promise for the future nor Abe's response made a real dent in her consciousness.

Her strength was beginning to return, but in her mind she felt defeated. Her usual habit of making plans was foreign to this strange person that lived in her body. She planned not at all, not even from hour to hour.

"Abe," directed the doctor, "give her all the buttermilk and eggs and good fresh vegetables she can eat. Once her body has healed, her spirit will follow. Of that I am sure!"

His manner was bluff and hearty, and he commanded attention. As he twisted his big body to struggle into his coat, he found in his pocket a telegram the postmaster had asked him to deliver.

"Maybe it's good news I have in my hand!" he boomed. "Open it up right away. It will do my heart good to see you smile again, Mrs. Hesse!"

But Susan knew better. She reached for the telegram, but then she waved it away, weakly, and gestured to Abe to open it.

"Susan," Abe said, as he was reading, "it's your father. He's gone. I'm sorry, Susan." He sat down next to her on the couch and took her hand. "That's just too bad. Too bad." His eyes sought hers but she avoided looking at him.

"Well," exclaimed Dr. Hosmer, "and so that's it! It's not good news at all." He sighed. "Not at all."

The shock was not as great as Susan might have expected. Over the last weeks she had prepared herself for this sad message and she absorbed its impact quietly.

But for the first time in several days she felt like doing something positive.

"Doc," she said, "Mama will need me now. If

Laura goes with me, do you suppose we could take the train over to the lake and then take the steamer? Maybe Mrs. Gerber could board the boys for a few days or her daughter Martha might stay there with Joseph until he finds a housekeeper.

"Maybe if I had the Spencer children trained, they could—?"

"Whoa! You're going too fast now, child. Another week, I'd say, before we hear anything like that!"

Susan realized Abe was still watching her intently, obviously not knowing what to make of her awakening. Her mind leapt feverishly from one idea to another. Somehow she must get away. Since her carefully laid plans had fallen apart, she had no desire to put her life here in order.

And once safely away, she knew she would never want to come back to this country that killed women and babies and men who were weak, even though they might have other admirable traits in abundance.

And where spirits that preyed on vulnerable victims drove them to practice various forms of superstition. That thought would have appalled her six months ago. Now it did not. The little rocker, having taken its toll, had been quiet all week. She wrenched her eyes away from it.

"But Mama needs me now," she said. "However will she get along during the next few weeks? Abe, you must send a message that I am on my way!"

Susan tossed back the lap robe and rose from the couch with no trouble. She ran lightly across the bedroom. Then she dragged her trunk from the far corner and threw open the top.

177

All at once her brain began to swim and she fell, exhausted, on the bed.

Abe stood in the doorway watching her, shaking his head sadly.

"Well, send the message anyway, Abe," she said. "Say I'll be there soon. And on the way, stop to see Laura. Tell her what I've decided to do."

Susan fell back onto her pillow and closed her eyes. Never before had she barked out orders to Abe—or to anyone else. But now her mouth seemed to say things in a certain way, with a certain tone, and she let the strange words take over.

"It's the weakness. That's all it is, my boy," she heard the doctor telling Abe out in the living room.

But Susan knew it was not her weakness that made her act this way. A part of her old rational, optimistic self was gone, and she had no wish to try to retrieve it.

A week later when Abe put her, along with Laura, on the train, she still had not tried to answer the questions in his eyes. She had kept the stance of a courteous stranger, a guest in the house. A guest who was grateful to her host for his kindness, but not desiring, indeed not even capable of anything remotely resembling affection.

Holding Susan's hand in his, after he had lifted her up to the door of the train on this hot August afternoon, Abe's face reflected a profound sadness, much like the sadness on the face of the Abe she had met early in the summer of the year before, just after Anna died.

But Susan's mind stubbornly refused to respond to him, even at the last. She just did not care.

CHAPTER 23

SUSAN'S LETHARGY HAD LASTED through the hot, dusty journey across the state and the boat ride on the gray swells of Lake Michigan. She and Laura sat wrapped in blankets on the deck of the steamboat and watched Milwaukee's low buildings come into focus on the horizon. A raw wind and low-hanging clouds kept most passengers inside. Now and then a man in a greatcoat and muffler braved the wind, but the rest chose comparative warmth—and seasickness.

Laura's worried questions had done little to arouse Susan. "When you see Mama," her sister finally said, "things will be better. You'll see."

"Mama's got her own problems," Susan could only murmur, and Laura was quiet again.

Adolph met them at the wharf. They saw him from the rail, holding his horse's halter and waving a white handkerchief to get their attention. The old man helped them off the boat and then fussed over the transfer of their trunk to a horse cart.

"What a time! What a time!" he said. "A bad time for you *kinder,* too, eh?"

"How is Mama?" Laura asked.

"As well as can be expected. She's a strong woman, your mama. They broke the mold, let me tell you. They broke the mold."

Susan remembered Mrs. Gerber's description of their mother's remarkable daughters. Maybe Mrs. Gerber was wrong after all.

She murmured a quiet, "And how are you, Uncle Adolph?" before she climbed into his buggy. "It was kind of you to stay for a while with Mama," she added. And then she sank back and closed her eyes. She had slept—or dozed—most of the day, during the past week.

A cool, pleasant breeze fanned her face, and soon she was asleep again.

Only when Susan woke and saw her mother's white frame house did she finally break down. But her weeping was all over by the time the buggy had traveled up the long driveway and reached the house. The familiar whispering poplars and the great fir tree in the front yard welcomed her.

Out of the corner of her eye she saw Adolph and Laura glancing at each other when she finally raised her chin and set her mouth tightly. She dried a few tears with her handkerchief.

"Oh, Laura," Susan cried, "I'm glad we're really home!"

Sinking into her own bed that night, with sensations

and scents of comfort all about her—carpets, draperies, and roast beef and pastries in the kitchen— she tried to sort out her impressions of the day.

Surely her mother was in mourning, but now Susan began to realize what a burden her father's illness had been, and how relieved her mother was to be free of it.

Susan and Laura had joined their mother and Adolph on the porch in the warm, early September evening. A robin sang in a big poplar, and the breeze brought smells of ripening apples in the orchard.

Already Susan's mother was planning well into the future. "There's a piece of land I heard about yesterday when the parson came to call. Now that I've finally finished with your poor Papa, I believe I will drive out to look it over in a day or two," she had said. Then she glanced toward Susan, who could not contain her astonishment. *Finally finished with Papa,* she thought.

Her mother stopped short for a moment before she took a quick breath and went on, briskly. "Now you must tell me more about poor Olive and those *kinder* she left," she said. "Are they going to grow up to be peasants, or is Joseph rearing them in a manner fit to bear his family name? I hope you set a good example for them yourself, Laura."

"Oh, Mama, Mama—" Laura began, but then she paused, her eyes imploring Susan to explain. Susan said nothing. There would be time in days to come, she knew, to let their mother start to understand what Olive's life had really been like. They need not talk about it during a homecoming.

Tossing about and unable to sleep, Susan thought,

181

Mama always looks ahead. Even now. Maybe that was the secret of the pioneers' strength. And she—who had been so confident only a few months before—had failed.

All at once she wondered what Abe was doing. Was he looking at those blank lines in the Bible, the way he so often did when he took it down to read at bedtime?

Was the chair rocking? Was that how Abe felt his sister's presence, too—by the movement of the chair that, she was convinced, had killed their baby?

Now Abe was alone and lonely again. Susan sighed, shifting her body restlessly once more in a bed that seemed large and empty.

Susan wondered if she were strong enough to return—ever—to Abe and to help him manage his farm and his life. Or if possibly his strength would be enough for both of them. Why was she thinking thoughts like these on her first night at home?

Where was her home?

I'm afraid, though, she told herself, *if I ever did go back, I'd always have to share our house with Anna, and not try to keep her out. Anna is a part of that house. And a part of Abe, too.*

Finally she drifted off into a fitful sleep.

"Now that you're rested, we'll all go into Milwaukee and hear Papa's will read," Susan's mother said the morning after Adolph went back to Chicago. "Surely Papa left nothing important for a rich man like his brother. A trinket or two, perhaps. Nothing more."

She was filling their hand-painted breakfast plates

with pancakes and sausages. Late pears and rich sour-cream-filled kuchen glistened in the lamplight from the center of the table.

"We can spend the night with Elviry," her mother went on. "Did I tell you girls what a tower of strength she's been for me in all my worry? She only just went back home before you got here. All that helping out with Papa at the last! And then she stayed on, too. Kind relations mean a lot in time of trouble, children."

She looked them over and Susan somehow felt a little guilty for not having come back when her mother needed her.

"Elviry'll be happy to see you girls, too," she added, having made her point.

Already the guilt feelings her mother had long inspired in her children were beginning to irritate Susan.

"I suppose Papa's will remembered the people in Prussia," said Laura.

Her mother gave her daughter a stern look. Obviously it was hard for her to begin to think of Laura as a young adult. "We'll see, child. We'll see," she said. "He changed it at the last, after Olive went, but he wouldn't tell me what he decided. He was hard to talk to these last weeks, your poor Papa."

Susan's old feeling about her father returned, too. *He was always hard to talk to,* she said to herself. Then she breathed a fleeting prayer for forgiveness. One must not think ill of the dead. But she *would* like to speak her mind to her mother. Just once.

Susan sat musing sadly in a chair by the window while her mother's new hired girl cleared the breakfast

183

dishes off the table and took them to the kitchen. The frail girl, the youngest of a neighbor's large family, was Laura's age, and she had been apprenticed out to learn household skills and good manners. Susan had planned to do the same for the orphaned Spencer children.

Now what would happen to them? Wearily she closed her mind to that problem in her old life.

But then, for a third time, she unfolded and read the letter from Abe that Adolph had brought from the South Milwaukee post office the day before. Abe must have written it only a few hours after she had left him. She could almost see him working over the letter, in his slow, deliberate way, at the kitchen table. First he would fold back her white linen cloth. He would pause from time to time to think things over as he began to write:

Dear Susan,

Please convey my sympathy to your mother.

Already, Susan, I miss you. And it has been only a little while since I saw you off on that train to Milwaukee. But ever since we lost our baby, I knew things were bad with you.

It was hard for you, Susan, a hard time, and I guess I was too busy a lot of the days these last months to help you out much.

Tonight I went over to see Joseph. He wants to go back to the town where he grew up. Joseph's older brother is dying in Prussia. He has business to see to over there, since he will inherit the family property, as you know. Joseph is in no condition to make plans for the little boys, so I told him you and I will care for them.

Susan, I did this without asking you. I know if we have the children with us, it will mean more work for you. But we will have the Spencer young folks with us to help out, too.

And I did something else without asking for your advice. Joseph said he would feel free to leave the boys only if they could stay there in their own home.

He said he will rent his house and his farmland to us until he gets back.

So, Susan, you will have a good house to live in when you get back here to your own family—with a cistern and a well by the kitchen door. In the meantime we will work to make our own house more comfortable for you to enjoy in the future. After Joseph returns. I hope you can soon let me know when you will be able to come back. I hope you are feeling well again by now.

I do not want to press you. But Joseph will be waiting for your answer, too.

Yr affectionate husband,

Abe

Susan lingered once more over the words *I miss you, when you come back,* and *yr affectionate husband,* and then she folded the letter. She went upstairs to her old room to dress in a black wool suit for the drive into Milwaukee. The intertwining leaves and flowers in the wallpaper that she had loved to follow just before sleep in past years now seemed to create only a perplexing, wearying puzzle for her tired eyes.

Susan and her mother and sister rode into town in a buggy pulled by a spirited roan mare. Her mother held the mare well in check. It was the way she always drove.

The first signs of fall were all about them—in the red, late-summer weeds along the dusty road, in the dawn, and in the long shadows of trees that crossed the roadway until mid-morning.

Their lawyer lived on the south side of Milwaukee, so they did not have to go through the city. He had his office in his home, a three-story house.

The lawyer's office was in a room that had been a front parlor. On his desk and on several tables sprawled untidy stacks of law books and legal papers. Heavy brown draperies covered three floor-to-ceiling windows, so the only light came from a small, dirty window high in one corner and from a fly-specked kerosene lamp with a great flowered globe that sat precariously on one corner of the big oak desk.

A slightly acrid odor from old books, old furnishings, and the unwashed old man filled the stuffy room.

"Do sit down and rest yourselves, ladies," he said in a gravelly voice, pulling up three walnut armchairs to the front of his desk.

After preliminaries, including a small glass of white wine for each of them, the lawyer put on his spectacles to read the will. He smoothed back his straggly white hair, cleared his throat, and began.

Susan expected nothing. "It's Karl who will inherit," declared Laura as soon as she'd heard the news of her father's death. "He has to finish his education. And maybe there will be something for Olive's boys." Susan recalled thinking then about Joseph's wealth and the fact that the boys could do well on their own.

186

She hardly listened to the legal language that allowed her mother the house and furniture and the income from a small hotel, along with some other properties.

There was a certain amount for the church and for the Lutheran school the girls had attended.

All the rest went to Karl except—except? Could she believe her ears? A thousand dollars for little Karl and for the baby. And a thousand dollars for each of his three remaining daughters—two in the United States and one in Prussia.

Susan looked at Laura and gasped. Had Laura heard the same thing? Laura's eyes were shining. *She* could continue her studies, too, the way Karl had. Maybe even in Berlin.

Susan's dream climbed out of the high window behind the lawyer's dusty, cluttered desk and across the miles.

She saw a well with a windmill next to her own sturdy barn-house, now painted a brilliant white, and a cistern, with a pump above it in the kitchen. The carpenter in the village could finish the attic and save Abe weeks of work.

The house would be filled with people. Live people that would crowd out unhealthy vapors and nightmares.

And, she thought, *who knows what next year might bring? Maybe I'll start taking music lessons again, with the piano teacher in the village. I'll even be used to living in that swampy land and maybe the ague won't bother me so much.*

She jumped to her feet. "Where," she asked the

lawyer, "is the nearest place I can arrange to send a message to my husband? I must tell him about my father's will!"

Susan was briefly aware of her mother's head bending over the legal papers on the desk, ignoring everyone else in the room, and of Laura, too, with her head in the clouds, unaware of anything but her own dreams.

"You drive on to Aunt Elviry's, Mama," she called, as she ran down the driveway toward the street the lawyer had pointed out. "I'll walk over as soon as I've written to Abe!"

One more resolve she made on her way down the street.

The first thing I will buy, even before I leave Milwaukee, is a rocking chair of my own. A beautiful, carved cherry rocker. And I will embroider a pillow for it. A green pillow with colors to match Uncle Adolph's carriage robe.

Suddenly she stopped beneath a tree to catch her breath. The warm sun filtered through its leaves, already becoming sparser than a week before. The dry grass smelled warm and kind. Late summer asters smiled at her from the lawn where the tree stood. The first deep blue sky of autumn bent like a benediction over her after the turmoil of the hot, angry skies she had known during the summer.

A solution, a happy solution, sprang directly into the cauldron of her plans.

And I can give Anna's rocking chair to the pastor for old ladies to sit in at the back of the church, so they won't have to try to keep from falling asleep on those hard benches. Granny Hosmer would be a match for any stray spirit! Abe would approve of my doing that with Anna's chair, I'm sure. And even Anna might be content.

The irrationality of the fact that she was trying to consider what Anna would want flitted only briefly across her mind. The solution was a good one. Anna's presence as a reality for Abe she might be able to put up with, but not her rocking chair. In *that* living room.

Starting back down the street, Susan formed the message for Abe in her mind.

"Coming home for good," she would say. "My home is with you."

Only later, on her way to Elviry's, did she realize she had forgotten to tell Abe about the inheritance.

CHAPTER 24

SUSAN'S ENTHUSIASM COOLED during the hours she traveled back across Michigan. There were only a few other passengers on the train. Her mother had bought a ticket for her daughter that allowed her some comfort, in a car with red-velvet-covered seats rather than the bench-lined car Abe was able to afford.

She began to think about her life in the years ahead without Olive—or even Laura—to talk to.

And one time when she laid her head back and dozed off, she dreamed about her living room. It was dusk there, a kind of pearly dusk. Anna's chair, with an elusive dark figure rocking in it, seemed to mock her homecoming. Wild laughter filled the room while the chair rocked faster and faster. She woke to find the train accelerating as it rattled down a steep grade. Susan stayed awake for the rest of the journey.

Abe met her at the station. "I took a chance on coming today to see if you might be along," he said.

Abe wore his black suit. He had brushed his coat and trimmed the mustache he had begun to grow to underscore his new identity as a married householder and prosperous farmer.

The smile that slowly lighted his whole face worked its old magic on Susan.

"Abe," she said, laughing, "you've washed the buggy! Was it just for me? If it was, I'm impressed!"

He put his hands on her shoulders and looked intently into her face. "Let's get in that buggy and go down the road where we can be private," he said. Susan was conscious of heads turning toward them. She wondered what stories people had heard about Abe's new wife's leaving the way she had.

Abe put her carpetbag on the floor of the buggy. "I'll come back for your trunk and that new chair you brought along tomorrow," he said.

A half-mile outside the village, be stopped the horse and wound the reins on the whip post. Then he put his arms around her and hugged her to him in a way he never had before. His mouth on hers was hungry.

She found herself responding eagerly, wanting more.

It was Abe, finally, who said, "Susan, Doc Hosmer says we'll have to wait awhile. Did you forget what he told you?"

She had. And in her new wisdom she realized she must follow the doctor's advice.

But it was Abe who remembered—and was looking out for her. She wanted to sing. To get out on the road and dance! She managed to swallow her exuberance and after a moment, she began to talk to him about the will and about her plans for the future.

Their drive along the road in golden September sunshine made a lie of memories of mud and mist and violent summer storms. Sumac beside the split-rail fences was turning red and cornflowers made a carpet of blue for bees and dragonflies. The clay earth smelled warm and fragrant.

When they reached their house Abe said, "Now I want you to lie down while I do the chores. I've got supper all planned for us. Mrs. Gerber brought over a custard. She said it was a homecoming present for you. Tomorrow we'll go to see Joseph. But for tonight, Susan, you just rest."

"At least I can gather eggs," Susan offered.

"Not one step outside the house!" he said.

Susan smiled. "That's an order?"

Abe laughed and looked at her happily for a long moment. Then he came around the buggy to help her down. "No, Susan," he said, "no orders from me." He opened the kitchen door. "But I do want you to lie down now. Will you?"

Susan took off her bonnet and glanced around the kitchen, bright in the clear late-afternoon sunshine. Through the door to the living room she could see her piano and the two rocking chairs. Abe had built a fire in the little stove in the living room. It looked inviting in there—warm and friendly. She *was* awfully tired.

"Well, since you insist," she said, "I guess I *will* lie on the couch until you come back from the barn. It's cozy with a nice fire. That was thoughtful, Abe." She smiled at him. "It's the first time we've used the living room stove."

192

Abe built the fire back up. He brought two wealthy apples from a crate on the porch for her. Then he changed into an old cotton shirt and patched trousers. He put on the work shoes he had left next to the door by the wood box.

"I might be quite a while," he said. "There's a lot I have to do."

Susan sighed, contented, as she lay on Adolph's red lap robe. She had brought a quilt from the bedroom. It still smelled of sweet herbs she had put into the rinse water when she washed it a month before.

The room was quiet. Anna's small pine rocker looked like any other rocking chair here in the country—comfortable and a little shabby. *Could it have been all in my mind?* she thought.

But she turned her face to the wall, away from the chair, before she dropped off into a deep sleep.

Susan awoke to the smell of smoke swirling across the ceiling of the darkening room. She choked, trying to see if the way to the door was clear. Flames crackled overhead along the hot stovepipe and sparks spurted out of a hole in its worn metal. On the far side of the room a small part of the ceiling fell. Then all at once a blazing corner of the floor of the attic came down, crashing into her piano.

Somehow unable to move or to take her streaming eyes away, she watched in horror as the flames engulfed her piano. They devoured the piece of furniture next to the piano, too—the little pine rocking chair. Thick smoke poured through the hole in the ceiling.

With a great effort Susan shut her eyes for an instant

193

and broke the spell. Frantically she tossed Adolph's robe over her head and scrambled off the couch. Holding her breath as long as she could, she crouched and felt her way along the wall to the kitchen door.

It was closed.

Never had the door to the kitchen been closed since she flung it open in the spring, vowing on that long-ago morning to challenge the rocking chair.

Gasping for air with her head inside the wool blanket, Susan fumbled for the handle. When she opened the door, a gust of hot air bore her through it—partly protected by her wrapping—and flung her into the kitchen.

Somehow she picked herself up and reached the back door. She stumbled down the porch steps and out into the yard, throwing the smoldering blanket away as she began to run. She raced to the well by the barn and immediately poured water from a bucket over her head. Her hair gave off an acrid odor as it fell over her face and around her shoulders.

Coughing up smoke and sobbing, she fell to her hands and knees. Then she lost consciousness.

She came back to awareness with Abe's arms around her.

"Oh, Susan, Susan, I was afraid you couldn't get out," he said, holding her tightly. "After I finished the chores, I went into the house and closed the kitchen door so you would be warm." He paused and smoothed her hair away from her face. "After that I saddled Dick and rode over to Joseph's. I told him we'd talk to him in the morning. And then when I got back out to the road I saw the fire."

Susan became aware of running shadowy figures and voices of shouting men. Several of the men, carrying buckets and large cans, were trying to form a line from the well to the house.

With tears streaming down her face she held onto Abe.

"Susan, are you sure you're all right?" Abe asked, peering into her face through the glare from the fire.

Her head was clearing, and although the taste of smoke still rose dark in her throat she knew at last she was really all right.

EPILOGUE

A DECEMBER GALE tore at the snug windows of Susan's house. There had been sleet in the morning, but now snow was piling great drifts across the path to the barn—Joseph's barn.

Joseph, having been taken ill during his Atlantic crossing, had not long survived his older brother.

While Susan set the table for supper, she watched little Karl Braun playing under their Christmas tree with a train made of spools.

Von Braun was an appellation neither she nor Abe would inflict on this American child.

Susan had written a Christmas letter to her mother: "Every day Abe and I realize we think the same way about important things. We want a good life for all the children under our roof.

"We had sorrows and worries this past year—every one of us. There were terrible worries I did not always write about in my letters, Mama. There were things I imagined, too, because I was lonely and life seemed

197

hard. Now we are thankful we can all be here together in this fine house Joseph left us. This house has sad memories for us, but it has happy ones, too.''

Abe had cleared away the charred remains of their little barn-house across the fields. "It's the end of a chapter in our lives, Susan," he had told her. "For me—that night put Anna to rest, I think. Now we can begin a new life—with Olive's babies—and, someday soon, our own. And when I think I nearly lost you, too—that night showed me that I need *you*, Susan. I need you for my wife.''

She turned from her work at the table to look again at a large red package under the looping strands of popcorn and cranberries on the tree. Mrs. Gerber had bought a new family Bible for Susan when she visited her daughter in the city. The Bible would be Susan's Christmas present to Abe. *Living with Abe is not like the way people lived in those novels I read in school,* she thought. *Husbands and wives don't always have to keep saying "I love you." I guess they just live it. And Abe lives his love every day.*

Then she heard Abe and Andy Spencer stamping their feet on the porch floor to get the snow off their boots.

"But I do love you, Abe," she said aloud. "And you," she repeated, dropping down by the tree to hug Karl. "And you," she called softly to Olive's sleeping baby and to Clara Spencer, who was folding diapers in the bedroom off the kitchen, and to Andy.

"And I love you, too," Susan breathed, her thoughts crossing the snowy fields to a tiny group of graves on a back road.

MEET THE AUTHOR . . .

ELAINE WATSON is an English instructor at Henry Ford Community College in Dearborn, Michigan. She has published numerous articles, and her poetry has appeared in various journals and magazines and in five anthologies. Mrs. Watson and her husband, who teaches history, have three children.

Anna's Rocking Chair recreates a nineteenth-century way of life that might be lost without the efforts of those who attempt to preserve it through art and literature. In this book, Mrs. Watson hopes to show that the hardships of the early settlers sometimes caused tension and illness that could be survived by only the strongest. This strength was derived, then as it is today, from staunch religious faith and innate common sense.

A Letter To Our Readers

Dear Reader:

Pioneering is an exhilarating experience, filled with opportunities for exploring new frontiers. The Zondervan Corporation is proud to be the first major publisher to launch a series of inspirational romances designed to inspire and uplift as well as to provide wholesome entertainment. In order that we might better contribute to your reading enjoyment, we would appreciate your taking a few minutes to respond to the following questions and return to:

Anne Severance, Editor
Serenade/Saga Books
749 Templeton Drive
Nashville, Tennessee 37205

1. Did you enjoy reading ANNA'S ROCKING CHAIR?

   ☐ Very much. I would like to see more books by this author!
   ☐ Moderately
   ☐ I would have enjoyed it more if _____

2. Where did you purchase this book? _____

3. What influenced your decision to purchase this book?

   ☐ Cover   ☐ Back cover copy
   ☐ Title   ☐ Friends
   ☐ Publicity   ☐ Other _____

4. Please rate the following elements (from 1 to 10):

☐ Heroine   ☐ Plot
☐ Hero   ☐ Inspirational theme
☐ Setting   ☐ Secondary characters

5. Which settings do you prefer?

_____   _____

_____   _____

6. What are some inspirational themes you would like to see treated in future Serenade books?

_____   _____

_____   _____

7. Would you be interested in reading other Serenade/Serenata or Serenade/Saga Books?

☐ Very interested
☐ Moderately interested
☐ Not interested

8. Please indicate your age range:

☐ Under 18   ☐ 25–34   ☐ 46–55
☐ 18–24   ☐ 35–45   ☐ Over 55

9. Would you be interested in a Serenade book club? If so, please give us your name and address:

Name _____

Occupation _____

Address _____

City _____ State _____ Zip _____

Serenade Saga Books are inspirational romances in historical settings, designed to bring you a joyful, heart-lifting reading experience.

Serenade Saga books available in your local bookstore: